No Sweetness Here
and Other Stories

Also by Ama Ata Aidoo

No Sweetness Here
and Other Stories

Ama Ata Aidoo

Afterword by Ketu H. Katrak

The Feminist Press
at The City University of New York
New York

Published 1995 by The Feminist Press at The City University of New York
365 Fifth Avenue, New York, NY 10016.
feministpress.org

04 03 02 01 00   6 5 4 3

Library of Congress Cataloging-in-Publication Data

Aidoo, Ama Ata, 1942–

    No sweetness here and other stories / Ama Ata Aidoo;
afterword by Ketu H. Katrak.

        p. cm.

    ISBN 1-55861-118-5. — ISBN 1-55861-119-3 (alk. paper)

    1. Ghana—Social life and customs—Fiction.   2. Short
stories, Ghanaian (English) I. Title.

PR9379.9.A35N6 1995

823—dc20   95-18346

                                 CIP

Front Cover: Adapted from Adinkra cloth, The Textile Museum,
Washington D.C. (1970.18.1), gift of Franklin H. Williams.

"Everything Counts" was first published in *Zuka;* "In the Cutting
of a Drink" in *Flamingo: The Message in Writing Today in Africa;*
"Certain Winds from the South" and "No Sweetness Here" in
Black Orpheus; "A Gift from Somewhere" in *Journal of New African
Literature,* "The Late Bud" in *Okyeame,* and "Other Versions" in *The
New African.* "Two Sisters" was first recorded as a short radio play
by The Transcription Centre, London.

This publication is made possible, in part, by public funds from the
National Endowment for the Arts and the New York State Council
on the Arts, and by a grant from the John D. and Catherine T.
MacArthur Foundation. The Feminist Press would also like to
thank Mariam Chamberlain, Helene Goldfarb, Joanne Markell,
Virginia L. Snitow, Judy Pigott Swenson, Caroline Urvater, and
Genevieve Vaughan for their generosity.

Cover design by Tina R. Malaney

Printed in the United States on acid-free paper by McNaughton &
Gunn, Inc., Saline, Michigan.

Contents

For those without whom living would have
been almost impossible

Everything Counts

She used to look at their serious faces and laugh silently to herself. They meant what they were saying. The only thing was that loving them all as sister, lover and mother, she also knew them. She knew them as intimately as the hems of her dresses. That it was so much easier for them to talk about the beauty of being oneself. Not to struggle to look like white girls. Not straightening one's hair. And above all, not to wear the wig.

The wig. Ah, the wig. They say it is made of artificial fibre. Others swear that if it is not gipsy hair, then it is Chinese. Extremists are sure they are made from the hairs of dead white folk – this one gave her nightmares, for she had read somewhere, a long time ago, about Germans making lampshades out of Jewish people's skins. And she would shiver for all the world to see. At other times, when her world was sweet like when she and Fiifi were together, the pictures that came into her mind were not so terrible. She would just think of the words of that crazy *highlife* song and laugh. The one about the people at home scrambling to pay exorbitant prices for second-hand clothes from America . . . and then as a student of economics, she would also try to remember some other truths she knew about Africa. Second-rate experts giving first-class dangerous advice. Or expressing uselessly fifth-rate opinions. Second-hand machinery from someone else's junkyard.

Snow-ploughs for tropical farms.

Outmoded tractors.

Discarded aeroplanes.

And now, wigs – made from other people's <u>unwanted hair</u>.

At this point, tough though she was, tears would come into her eyes. Perhaps her people had really missed the boat of original thinking after all? And if Fiifi asked her what was wrong, she explained, telling the same story every time. He always shook his head and laughed at her, which meant that in the end, she would laugh with him.

At the beginning, she used to argue with them, earnestly. 'But what has wearing wigs got to do with the revolution?' 'A lot sister,' they would say. 'How?' she would ask, struggling not to understand.

'Because it means that we have no confidence in ourselves.' Of course, she understood what they meant.

'But this is funny. Listen, my brothers, if we honestly tackled the problems facing us, we wouldn't have the time to worry about such trifles as wigs.'

She made them angry. Not with the mild displeasure of brothers, but with the hatred of wounded lovers. They looked terrible, their eyes changing, turning red and warning her that if she wasn't careful, they would destroy her. Ah, they frightened her a lot, quite often too. Especially when she thought of what filled them with that kind of hatred.

This was something else. She had always known that in her society men and women had had more important things to do than fight each other in the mind. It was not in school that she had learnt this. Because you know, one did not really go to school to learn about Africa. . . . As for this, what did the experts call it? War of the sexes? Yes, as for this war of the sexes, if there had been any at all in the old days among her people, they could not possibly have been on such a scale. These days, any little 'No' one says to a boy's 'Yes' means one is asking for a battle. O, there just are too many problems.

As for imitating white women, mm, what else can one

do, seeing how some of our brothers behave? The things one has seen with one's own eyes. The stories one has heard. About African politicians and diplomats abroad. But then, one has enough troubles already without treading on big toes.

After a time, she gave up arguing with them, her brothers. She just stated clearly that the wig was an easy way out as far as she was concerned. She could not afford to waste that much time on her hair. The wig was, after all, only a hat. A turban. Would they please leave her alone? What was more, if they really wanted to see a revolution, why didn't they work constructively in other ways for it?

She shut them up. For they knew their own weaknesses too, that they themselves were neither prepared nor ready to face the realities and give up those aspects of their personal dream which stood between them and the meaningful actions they ought to take. Above all, she was really beautiful and intelligent. They loved and respected her.

She didn't work that hard and she didn't do brilliantly in the examinations. But she passed and got the new degree. Three months later, she and Fiifi agreed that it would be better for them to get married among a foreign people. Weddings at home were too full of misguided foolishness. She flew home, a month after the wedding, with two suitcases. The rest of their luggage was following them in a ship. Fiifi would not be starting work for about three months so he had branched off to visit some one or two African countries.

Really, she had found it difficult to believe her eyes. How could she? From the air-stewardesses to the grade-three typists in the offices, every girl simply wore a wig. Not cut discreetly short and disguised to look like her own hair as she had tried to do with hers. But blatantly, aggressively, crudely. Most of them actually had masses of flowing curls falling on their shoulders. Or huge affairs piled on top of their heads.

Even that was not the whole story. Suddenly, it seemed as if all the girls and women she knew and remembered as having

3

smooth black skins had turned light-skinned. Not uniformly. Lord, people looked as though a terrible plague was sweeping through the land. A plague that made funny patchworks of faces and necks.

She couldn't understand it so she told herself she was dreaming. Maybe there was a simple explanation. Perhaps a new god had been born while she was away, for whom there was a new festival. And when the celebrations were over, they would remove the masks from their faces and those horrid-looking things off their heads.

A week went by and the masks were still on. More than once, she thought of asking one of the girls she had been to school with, what it was all about. But she restrained herself. She did not want to look more of a stranger than she already felt – seeing she was also the one *black* girl in the whole city. . . .

Then the long vacation was over and the students of the national university returned to the campus. O . . . she was full of enthusiasm, as she prepared her lectures for the first few weeks. She was going to tell them what was what. That as students of economics, their role in nation-building was going to be crucial. Much more than big-mouthed, big-living politicians, they could do vital work to save the continent from the grip of its enemies. If only for a little while: and blah, blah, blah.

Meanwhile, she was wearing her own hair. Just lightly touched to make it easier to comb. In fact, she had been doing that since the day they got married. The result of some hard bargaining. The final agreement was that any day of the year, she would be around with her own hair. But she could still keep that thing by for emergencies. Anyhow, the first morning in her life as a lecturer arrived. She met the students at eleven. They numbered between fifteen and twenty. About a third of them were girls. She had not seen them walk in and so could not tell whether they had beautiful bodies or not. But lord, were their faces pretty? So she wondered as she stared, open-mouthed at them, how she would have felt if she had been a young male. She smiled momentarily at herself for the silliness of the idea. It was a mistake to stop the smile. She should just have gone on and developed it into a laugh. For close at its heels was a jealousy so big, she did not know what to do with it. Who were these girls? Where had they come from to confront her with their youth? The fact that she wasn't really that much older than any of them did not matter. Nor even that she recognised one or two who had come as first years, when she was in her fifth year. She remembered them quite clearly. Little skinny greenhorns scuttling timidly away to do her bidding as the house-prefect. Little frightened lost creatures from villages and developing slums who had come to this citadel of an alien culture to be turned into ladies. . . .

And yet she was there as a lecturer. Talking about one thing or another. Perhaps it was on automation as the newest weapon from the industrially developed countries against the wretched ones of the earth. Or something of the sort. Perhaps since it was her first hour with them, she was only giving them general ideas on what the course was about.

Anyhow, her mind was not there with them. Look at that one, Grace Mensah. Poor thing. She had cried and cried when she was being taught to use knives and forks. And now look at her.

It was then she noticed the wigs. All the girls were wearing them. The biggest ones she had seen so far. She felt very hot and she who hardly ever sweated, realised that not only were her hands wet, but also streams of water were pouring from the nape of her neck down her spine. Her brassiere felt too tight. Later, she was thankful that black women have not yet learnt to faint away in moments of extreme agitation.

But what frightened her was that she could not stop the voice of one of the boys as it came from across the sea, from the foreign land, where she had once been with them.

'But Sissie, look here, we see what you mean. Except that

5

it is not the real point we are getting at. Traditionally, women from your area might have worn their hair long. However, you've still got to admit that there is an element in this wig-wearing that is totally foreign. Unhealthy.'

Eventually, that first horrid lecture was over. The girls came to greet her. They might have wondered what was wrong with this new lecturer. And so probably did the boys. She was not going to allow that to worry her. There always is something wrong with lecturers. Besides, she was going to have lots of opportunities to correct what bad impressions she had created. . . .

The next few weeks came and went without changing anything. Indeed, things got worse and worse. When she went home to see her relatives, the questions they asked her were so painful she could not find answers for them.

'What car are you bringing home, Sissie? We hope it is not one of those little coconut shells with two doors, heh? . . . And oh, we hope you brought a refrigerator. Because you simply cannot find one here these days. And if you do, it costs so much. . . .' How could she tell them that cars and fridges are ropes with which we are hanging ourselves? She looked at their faces and wondered if they were the same ones she had longed to see with such pain, when she was away. Hmm, she began to think she was in another country. Perhaps she had come down from the plane at the wrong airport? Too soon? Too late? Fiifi had not arrived in the country yet. That might have had something to do with the sudden interest she developed in the beauty contest. It wasn't really a part of her. But there it was. Now she was eagerly buying the morning papers to look out for the photos of the winners from the regions. Of course, the winner on the national level was going to enter for the Miss Earth title.

She knew all along that she would go to the stadium. And she did not find it difficult to get a good seat.

She should have known that it would turn out like that. She had not thought any of the girls beautiful. But her opinions were not really asked for, were they? She just recalled, later, that all the contestants had worn wigs except one. The winner. The most light-skinned of them all. No, she didn't wear a wig. Her hair, a mulatto's, quite simply, quite naturally, fell in a luxuriant mane on her shoulders. . . .

She hurried home and into the bathroom where she vomited – and cried and cried and vomited for what seemed to her to be days. And all this time, she was thinking of how right the boys had been. She would have liked to run to where they were to tell them so. To ask them to forgive her for having dared to contradict them. They had been so very right. Her brothers, lovers and husbands. But nearly all of them were still abroad. In Europe, America or some place else. They used to tell her that they found the thought of returning home frightening. They would be frustrated. . . .

Others were still studying for one or two more degrees. A Master's here. A Doctorate there. . . . That was the other thing about the revolution.

For Whom Things
Did Not Change

Knock . . . knock . . . knock . . .
　'A-ha?'
　'Massa, Massa, Massa . . .'
　'A-ha? A-ha? A-ha?'
　'You say make I com' wake you. Make I com' wake you for
eight. Eight o'clock 'e reach.'
　'Okay, thank you.'
　Knock . . . knock . . . knock . . .
　'A-ha?'
　'Massa, Massa, Massa.'
　'A-ha? A-ha? A-ha?'
　'You say make I com' wake you. Make I com' wake you for
eight. Eight o'clock reach long time.'
　'Okay, thank you, Zirigu.'
　　　　　　　　·　·　·　·　·

'I think this is a strange one. This young master. You can see
he is very tired. But he insists that he should be woken up at
eight o'clock. And I wonder what he thinks he can do in a
place like this from that hour. He must be one of these people
who don't know how to rest. Even when they are scholars.'
　'Zirigu my husband, sometimes you talk as though it is not
yourself speaking but some child. Do you think people are
all the same because they all went to school and are big
masters?'

'Setu, you know I do not think anything like that. But you must agree that after all these years, I can say something about the type of human beings who come here. This young one seems different.'

'And what is the difference?'

'Ah-ah. He does not drink at all. He has never asked me to serve him with anything strong or buy him any from the town.'

'Maybe he is a Believer?'

'No-no. He is from the coast. And I have not met many big men from those areas who are Moslems. But that is not what I mean really. Most of the Believers from your area who are big men are not different from the others. Yes, they do not drink – some do even that – but then, that is all. They are all like the others.'

'As for me, what I have just noticed is that he did not bring a woman with him.'

'*Eh-heh!* Ah Setu, so you know what I mean?'

'What do I know?'

'That this one is different?'

'Maybe. He certainly did not bring one of those nasty pieces with their heads swollen outside and inside like the meat and feathers of overfed turkeys. Ah, Allah!'

'What is it, Setu?'

'Zirigu, I am thinking of those girls.'

'My wife, it is because you have nothing to do. Are you not making kaffa to take to the market today?'

'No. I have no meal left. And I thought my ears were aching too much last night. Allah knows I have debts like everyone else. But since they will not come and kill me if I do not pay them this morning, I think I shall rest today from carrying agidi; and maybe go and see the doctor. After all, how much does one make?'

'Hm, hm! And so this is why you have got all this time and mouth to talk about those girls?'

'Yes. And I think they are a pain. Oh you do not think so,

B

my husband? Do not shake your head with that glint in your eyes as though I a.n mad for talking like this. Do they not come from homes? Have they not got fathers and mothers?'

'What are you saying, Setu?'

'I'm saying, Zirigu, that there must be something wrong when young girls who have seen their blood not many moons gone, go sleeping with men who are old enough to be their fathers, and sometimes their grandfathers. And no one is saying anything. Look, look, ho, ho, look. Everyone sees them on the land, and no one says anything.'

('But the men are big men. They have the money. They have all the nice things, like big cars and the false hair which come from the white man's land. And the little girls sleep with them because they like these things.')

'But what do the mothers of these little girls say?'

'What can they say? Some of them do not even know that their children are like this. They live in the villages and when their daughters take good things home, they think it is because they are ladies and have got them all with the pay from their work. Some clans learn from the wayside how their daughters are living in the cities. But they are afraid to say anything.'

'But why should anyone fear her own daughter?'

'Because she has got a big mouth from what she has seen.'

'Allah!'

'But my wife, that is not all. Sometimes they are not afraid of the daughter herself but the big man. Because he has big power and he can ruin them if they do not give him what he wants – their daughter. And Setu my wife, such things have been known to happen.'

'O Allah, what times we live in. What rulers we have. How can men behave in this way who are our lords?'

'Mm. Was it different in the old days, Setu my wife? Did not the lords take the little girls they liked among the women?'

'Zirigu, I do not know. I'm sure you are right. But Allah has made it so. All women are slaves of our lords. These new masters are not Believers. It is not Allah's will. And they are shameful acts.'

'But my wife, what are you saying? When a man is your lord, he is your lord. And he behaves like your lord. How else should he behave? And how are we to say that new lords must not do what old ones did? When the white men were here, did they not do the same? Sleep with very little girls, oh, such little girls?' Big Menlike Bridle.

'I do not know, Zirigu, I do not know, my husband. . . . Yes, I saw some of these things, when those people were here. But listen, my husband. If one day when you are not looking, a man comes and takes your farmhouse or your kraal, and he begins doing all the things a good man should not do; sells all the yams in your barns without leaving any for planting; boils your eggs as soon as they have been laid and does not spare one for a single hen to hatch; gives great feasts to all his family and all his friends, with your lambs and calves; and generally carries on in such a way that your heart hurts as though it is falling into your bowels every time you look on; and yet you are not able to do anything for many many years, but then one day, thanks to Allah, you get your farmhouse or your kraal back, what then do you do, my husband? So, from the first day, you too begin to kill or sell what is left of your old and miserable cows, sheep and chickens? And if an egg is just laid, you boil it right away, and generally continue the destruction of your property which that robber had started?'

'I do not know, Zirigu, but it is certainly good that all my children are boys. It is good I never had a daughter. Because if I had had a daughter, and I knew a big man was doing unholy things with her, then with a matchet in my own hand, I would have cut that big man to pieces myself!'

'Oh, Jesu preserve my soul. O Jesu! Setu, what kind of talk is this? You must pray more than everybody else on Friday for these foul words.'

'Yes, my husband. Let us thank Allah for what he gives. As I say, it is good I have no daughter.'

11

'Maybe it is better that all mothers are not like you. Otherwise the land would be flowing with the blood of all the big men.'

'And who shall lament to see the blood of evil men flow?'

'But since the masters of the land are always bad, or they have been bad for a long, long time, do you not know that people would not like to see the new ones die? They, like the daughters, also come from homes. Homes where people eat well because they know the big men. Do you think that everybody in the land is like you and me? No, my wife. There are people who will lament to see a big man killed. Because knowing a big man means having someone in the town who has a huge house. It means . . . but it is enough, my wife. The big men we saw yesterday were bad. These we see today are worse. And be sure that those of tomorrow will be like those of yesterday and today put together.'

'Stop, stop. Stop, Zirigu. You make me feel cold all of a sudden.'

'Women! Were you not the same Setu who, a while ago, was all ready to cut someone down with a matchet?'

'But what does one do?'

'How do I know? I serve them the drinks they ask, cook their meals if they want me to, make their beds, sweep their rooms, and more. And if they bring their women, look after them too. You know, my wife, as well as I, that that has been my life. As for the families of those things – as you call the little girls – that, my wife, I do not know.'

'Yes, Zirigu, now that you say it, I remember that not all of them, I mean their mothers, even disapprove.'

'Ah . . .'

'Look at that Munatu, girl.'

'Ah . . .'

'Do you know how those uncles of hers could have found the money to build that mansion?'

'Ah . . .'

'Twelve rooms; they say it has. Twelve rooms. And many pipes for government water in the house. And those who have been inside and peeped into some of the rooms, say that one must see them with one's own eyes to believe that there are women and men who have such rooms to sleep in.'

'Ah . . .'

'And so people try to profit by their daughters by giving them to the big men? And they sometimes even encourage them . . .?'

'Ah . . .'

'And if they are like that Munatu's mother, they come to the market-place telling everybody what and what my lord master is doing and saying . . .?'

'Ah . . .'

'When you know that the man will leave your daughter when he's tired of her or he sees another girl who is more beautiful?'

'Ah . . .'

'I spit upon such big men! I spit upon such mothers! I spit upon such daughters!'

'My wife, now that you are feeling better inside, I will leave you and go to wake up my young master.'

'And I am getting ready to go and see the doctor about my ears.'

. . . . .

Knock, knock, knock.

'Massa, Massa, Massa . . .'

'Y-e-s?'

'Massa, Massa, Massa.'

'Y-e-s?'

'You say: "Zirigu, wake me for eight." At eight, I com', you no wake. At 'a pas' eight, I com', you no wake. Now, you go wake because 'e be nine o'clock.'

'But Zirigu, the door was not locked. You could have come and dragged me out!'

13

'Ah, Massa, you make me laugh. Me, Zirigu, com' where yourself sleep com' pull you?'

'Why not?'

'I no fit.'

'Okay, we shall not argue further about it. Thank you for managing to get me up at last.'

'But weyting you think you fit do for this place so you wake up early so?'

'Nothing really. You are right. But I just want to keep on waking up early. It will be bad for me to get used to sleeping late. I should try to get up much earlier than this anyway, but I feel very tired so I am going slow.'

'But why? For Massa, you fit sleep late. Weyting you go do for office? Like me, I wake early, yes. But you, no!'

'Zirigu, not all educated people work in offices.'

'No?'

'No. And one of these days, I think I'm going to tell you why I don't want to get used to sleeping late.'

Christ I can feel it coming.

'I don' make you coffee for long time. Maybe now, 'e be cold, I go stand am for stove.'

'Take your time, man. I'll wash myself and then come and fetch it. Please Zirigu, I've said that you shouldn't wait on me hand and foot.'

'Massa!'

'Well, I don't see why you should. You are old enough to be my father.'

'My white Massa!'

'And I am not a white man.'

'Massa!'

'Listen, the kitchen is your territory and I shall not come and mess around there. Besides, I am a guest here so there are things I know I should not do. But I'll be damned if you are going to get me to behave as though I were some accursed invalid or something.'

'Lord, lord, Massa, such talk no fit for your mout'. I like

yourself so you fit do weyting you like. The sun don' com' up long time. I wan' go get good meat for you so I must hurry to market before twelve. Tell me what you sabe for breakfast make I do. Omelette? Poached eggs. Fried egg on toast. Eggs and bacon. Orange juice . . .'

'Stop, Zirigu!'

'Why, Massa?'

'I'm not having any breakfast. Have you got fresh oranges?'

'No? . . . Yes, in my wife's kitchen. I go bring am for you.'

'I will pay for it.'

'No fear. When I go for market, I go buy you better. Plenty Massas only drink orange juice for the bottle.'

'I'm mad but I think I'm sane enough not to drink pressed, homogenised, dehydrated, re-crystallised, thawed, diluted and heaven-knows-what-else orange juice, imported from countries where oranges do not grow, when I can eat oranges.'

'What you say, Massa?'

'Never mind, Zirigu.'

. . . . .

'If you ask them, why ten years after independence, some of us still have to be slaves, they say you are nuts to ask questions like that.'

'You are getting your definitions wrong. By what stretch of imagination does a steward-boy or a housemaid become a slave?'

'Was it not enough that whole sections of us were bred so that all they could do was to minister to the needs of white men and women? Doing soul-killing jobs? Do they have to do them for us too?'

'What are you talking about? It partially solves the unemployment problem. Or minimises it, at least. Can you imagine what would happen if all the house-boys and housemaids were not doing what they are doing?'

'How about the pay?'

'How about it?'

15

'And anyway, most of them, especially the house-girls, are people's relatives . . .'

'Problems are solved only when you tackle them in all seriousness.'

'Eh – captain, another beer, please.'

.   .   .   .   .

'Massa, I must go to market now. I say I wan' get good meat. What you go chop?'

'I'll eat anything you cook.'

'Massa, you tink you go like fried fillet of calf? Or a braised lamb liver? Yes, here a good one. An escalope of veal with onions and fried potatoes.'

'Zirigu, whom did you say you were going to cook for?'

'Yourself, Massa.'

'But that is not the food I eat.'

'But 'e be white man chop.'

'Zirigu, I no be white man. And that is the second time this morning I've told you that. And if you do it again, I'll pack up and leave.'

Jesus, isn't there anywhere on this bloody land one can have some blinking peace? Jesus . . . Lord I am sweating . . . God . . . see how I'm sweating. Jesus see how I'm sweating.

'Massa, why you sweat so?'

'It gets hot here early.'

'Yes, make I open them windows.'

Jesus!

'Massa, I beg. Don't make so. I no wan' vex you. This here chop, 'e be white man's chop. 'E be the chop I cook for all massas, for fifteen years. The Ministars, the party people who stay for here, the big men from the Ministries, the Unifartisy people, the big offisars from the army and police. . . . 'E be same chop, they chop, this white man chop.'

'Zirigu, can't you cook any food of the land? Don't they sell things in that market with which you could make the food of this land?'

16

'Yes. But I no fit cook your kind food. No, I no fit cook food of your area.'

'How about the food of your area? Your food?'

'I no fit cook that.'

'Jesus. And you've been a cook steward here for all these years?'

'Yes. But Massa. I know my job. Massa, don't com' make trouble for me. O, look, my hair don' gone white. I no fit find another job. Who go look for my pickin'? I know how to cook, Massa, white man's chop.'

'That's the problem. Listen. God forbid you should even think I'll make trouble for you. In fact, that is not what I am talking about. But I'm just about beginning to understand. Gradually. You went into training, qualified and have been gaining experience all these years as a cook for white people. You do not know how to cook the food of the land because it is your food. And you are a man. And a man normally does not cook. But you cook the white man's chop because that is white man's chop, your job, not food. Or . . .'

'Massa, God knows I know my job.'

'Of course! As a man of the land and your wife's husband you are a man and therefore you do not cook. As a black man facing a white man, his servant, you are a black, not a man, therefore you can cook.'

'Massa, Massa. You call me woman? I swear, by God, Massa, this na tough. I no be woman. God forbid!'

'Ah, Zirigu. I am only thinking something out. Ah . . . God is above, I no call you woman. Soon I go talk all for you.'

'But Massa, you no know. Don't call me woman.'

'No, I will not.'

. . . . .

When a black man is with his wife who cooks and chores for him, he is a man. When he is with white folk for whom he cooks and chores, he is a woman. Dear Lord, what then is a black man who cooks and chores for black men?

. . . . .

17

'Listen Zirigu, does the Mother your wife know how to cook the food of the land?'

'Yes. But not of your area.'

'No. Of your area.'

'Yes!'

'Okay, can you charge me the normal rate for supper and ask the Mother to count my mouth in for the supper this evening?'

'W-h-a-t? What you say Massa? What?'

'I say, Zirigu, can the Mother count my stomach in for the evening's meal?'

'Massa. I no wan' play?'

'I am not playing.'

'Heh? God. You mean you go eat *tuo*?'

'Why not? At home I eat *banku*. Isn't it the same? One of rice, the other of corn? Aren't they all farina? Semolina? Whatever?'

'Massa, I no wan' trouble.'

'What kind of trouble do you think you are going to get? Perhaps you think I'm a child?'

'I mean your tommy.'

'What about my tummy? Do you get tummy trouble when you eat your wife's food? What are you saying, man? And anyway, I can look after myself in that kind of way. I am a medical doctor, you know.'

'I know, young Massa. I say, this man look small but him too, 'e be big man. . . . But you go chop, *tuo*?'

'Yes.'

'As for you self!'

.   .   .   .   .   .

'S-e-t-u! S-e-t-u! S-e-t-u-e-e-e! Where is that woman? S-e-t-u!'

'What is it, Zirigu? I was in the bath. Did I not tell you I was getting ready to go and see the doctor?'

'Listen, my wife. I never heard a story like this before.'

18

'Well, I haven't either. But how can I know for sure when you are not telling it?'

'Hmm . . . S-e-t-u . . . how shall I begin?'

'Perhaps we better wait until this evening, since I have no time to . . .'

'No . . . no . . . no! Hmm Setu, the young Master says he does not want to eat this evening.'

'And is that a story?'

'But that is not all.'

'Well, just tell me the rest.'

'He says he will eat some of your food this evening!'

'*H-e-e-eh!* Allah. Zirigu, it is not true.'

'He is in there, sitting by the table eating his orange. Go and ask him.'

'*E-e-e* Allah. Zirigu, do you think this boy is right in his head? '

'Setu, I am not sure. Setu, really, I am not sure. But his eyes do not rove so even if he is ill, it is not serious yet. He talks funny sometimes though. But I don't know. Yes, he says he will eat *tuo* and that I can charge it to his general bill. Lord, in all the twenty or so years I've been general keeper and cook for this Rest House, I have not encountered a thing like this, eh Setu, have we?'

'No, my husband. But times do change.'

'Yes, you are right, my wife. So after you've been to see the doctor, go straight to the market, buy some very good vegetables, fresh greens, okro . . .'

'Zirigu, now you better shut up your mouth before you annoy me. Since when did you start teaching me how to do my marketing? This is my job. A woman's job.'

'Yes, Setu.'

. . . . .

'Massa . . .'

'Zirigu, how often should I tell you not to call me that?'

'But you are my massa!'

'I am nothing of the sort. I was born not six years when you were going away to fight. How can I be your massa? And this is a Government Rest House, not mine, I am not even your employer. So how can I be your Master?'

'But all the other Massas, they don't say make I no call them so?'

'Hell they don't. That is their business. Not mine. My name is Kobina, not Master.'

'Kob-i-n-a . . . K-o . . . Massa, I beg, I no fit call you that. I simple no fit.'

'Too bad. That means I'll have to leave here too, earlier than I had hoped.'

'I dey go for town buy eggs, soap and some more yama-yama for the house. Make I buy you something?'

'Oranges, more fruit.'

'No drink?'

'Christ, no. Ah, yes, perhaps *pito*?'

'As for you, Massa self! You wan' drink *pito*?'

'I want to taste it. I understand one can get it real fresh around here. And I want to taste it. Haven't drunk any before. Is it good? Does it make one drunk?'

'Yes. Very good. No, 'e no make one drunk. Not too mus.'

.   .   .   .   .

There should be something said for open spaces. And yet what? Nothing. It should be possible that if one can see several miles out in front, into the distance, one should also be able to see into time. All this breeze. These clear skies. Fresh breezes should blow the nonsense from our souls, the stupidities from our minds and lift the veils off our eyes. But it's not like that. It's never been like that. There are as many cramped souls around here as there are among the dwellers down there. In the thick woods and on the beaches. Like everyone else, those poets were wrong. They lied. But Zirigu is alright. And so is his wife, the Mother. They are alright, like all of us. Alright. I only hope that one day, they will learn that we are all the same.

One day, when I was tiny and I went to spend the holidays with Nanaa I pattered behind her to the farms. I can hear her now. 'Now, my young scholar, do not follow me: the farm is for seasoned ones like me. Hmm, how can I answer if anything goes wrong?' . . . And on and on and on. But I went all the same. All I remember is that everything just smelt like it had never done before – or since. Good. Good. Good. It was not just the smell of green leaves. Green leaves and wet earth, fire spilling from a gun and fresh-spilt human blood smell different, to be sure. At Nanaa's farm, things smelt good. All the vegetables were there. Anyway, we had been hardly an hour there when I began to holler for food. Nanaa muttered something about obviously that day on the farm going to be devoted to eating. And then she dashed behind some bush and came out with this huge yam. I mean it was big. A giant. Of course when you are young, even little things have a way of gaining size in your eyes, but this yam was big. She removed the little kerosene tin pot – they used to sell them for fourpence and sixpence in the market – from its hiding place and poured some water into it. At the sight of the yam my throat had begun doing what throats do. She had said she would cut just a little bit of the tip and cook it for me because she herself was not hungry, and anyway, yam is no good cold. All this sounded fine to me. It just meant that when she came to cook hers, I would have more yam to eat. I already knew that when yam is good it is white or whitish-yellow or something. But when Nanaa cut the piece it was brown. And she said something about that piece being no good. She cut another. It was the same. She cut another piece, it was not different. And she cut another and yet another. They were all the same. Somewhere at the middle, Nanaa looked at the yam and said, 'Yam, you really are wicked. Why didn't you leave a piece of yourself good when you were going bad, so I could have cooked you for my little master?' But I told her to cut on, for I still hoped

21

that all was not lost. So she turned the remaining piece round and cut out the head. It was brown and soft. I threw myself into the sand and dust of the farm and screamed. She cooked me a fresh piece from the barn, but I refused to eat it. It was only later when she boiled some for herself and by which time I was too hungry to refuse anyway, that I ate. And I have never forgotten about that yam. What was it that ate it up so completely? And yet, here I go again, old yam has to rot in order that new yam can grow. Where is the earth? Who is going to do the planting? Certainly not us – too full with drink, eyes clouded in smoke, and heads full of women . . . and our hearts desiring only nonsensical articles from someone else's factory. . . .

There was an air of festivity at the Rest House because I had said I was going to eat what Zirigu and his wife ate. The woman came to let me know, with the few words of my language she knew, that I should have given her adequate warning so she could have feasted me properly. I said that was okay because there was another day coming. Zirigu laid the table and when I told him that he should not give me a fork and a knife because I was going to eat with hands and that I only needed a spoon to scoop down the soup, he opened his mouth wide. When I was eating, both of them came to watch me. The food was alright. Of course, it tasted strange like anything else you are not used to. I could detect a not-too-familiar seasoning here, a foreign spice there. But on the whole there was nothing in the strangeness of it that I thought one could not get used to. I have eaten stranger meals. Zirigu let me know of just one anxiety he had. That my bowels would run in the night. Later, he brought the *pito*. I asked him to sit down and drink with me. He attempted to protest. One doesn't drink with the master, you know. I assured him it was alright. The wine was good. It has a sweetness in it. As we drank, we talked. I told him more about myself. He seemed to understand and sympathise. When we were through with my bottle, he said that he was going to bring one of his own.

He did. Gradually the main part of the talking switched to him.

. . . . .

'My young Master, forgive me for still addressing you like this. But then, is there anything else I can do? At my age, it is too late for me to start being too familiar with my betters. No, no, don't say any more. You are a good, young man. I like you. But really, how can I call you this Kobina? Yes, in years you are a baby. You don't have to tell me that. Can I not see that for myself? I can see that for myself. But now, age alone does not mean much, not much. It is a long time since age lost weight. In the old days, when a person was one day older than you, you had to defer to him or the whole clan would let you know your actual self, an insignificant miserable worm! But when your age does not prevent you from washing the underclothes of a white woman whom you know to be much much younger than yourself, what then is age? Thank God, I stopped doing that a long time ago. As for the black men who became the new masters when the white men went, well, they do not seem to think much of age either. I will tell you something soon. But even in the old times, people said that just to be old in itself was nothing. One could be old wise or old foolish. They used to say that to travel then was the thing. Well, my young master, I, Zirigu, I have travelled some. As I told you, I am an Ex-Serviceman. Went to Burma – or some place like that. Seen the front. But now you tell me you know what it is to be a soldier because you went to the Congo with our boys. Then I shall not tell you about the front. But it was there I learnt about white people. Oh, my young Master, when they are hungry, they can fight for food, and cheat each other like anybody else. . . . Sometimes you put food there for some people who were away. And their friends would eat it. When those people came back and there was nothing, they beat you. Yes, maybe, they would argue with their own brothers, but it was us they beat up. Hah, what man has seen!

'Of course, some of us fought. That's how people died. Or lost legs and arms. And to this day that I am talking to you, my Master, I don't know whom we were there fighting and why.

'You know book, my young Master, so to be sure, you've read all about the ex-Servicemen and the promises and how nothing was done. A few months after we came back and found ourselves demobilised many of us started going to pieces. I was afraid of not having anything to do for my living. With my friend – he was Setu's brother – I left the Gold Coast. Where have I not been in West Africa? Togoland? Nigeria? Sa'Lo? But everywhere it was the same, there were always too many ex-Servicemen already without jobs. I tried peddling, bicycle repairing, carpentering. . . . It was the same; emptiness behind and emptiness before. We came back. But one thing I forgot to tell you. Before I went to the war I was selling yam in the big market in Takoradi. It was a good trade. And when I was just about to leave, I gave the little money I had saved to my own brother. My father's child. My mother's child. I said to him: "Buda, keep this for me. If they do not kill me and I come back, I will still trade in yam. And maybe we will do it together because it is a good trade." My Master, I will not talk too long. Buda is my own brother. He came after me one year and a half from the same womb. When I returned home from the wars, he had eaten the money. Married a wife with some of it, and the two of them had eaten the rest of my money. You people over there think that all of us over here are thieves and murderers or something. But listen, when I didn't take a knife and cut my brother down, I know I can never kill anybody else in cold blood as long as they call me Zirigu. In fact, that was one reason why I left this land with Setu's brother. And we came back after six years, with nothing. At that time, both of us thought we were already getting too old. We heard there was a place somewhere in the big city where other ex-Servicemen were training to be cooks, steward-boys and garden-boys. I talked it over with Setu's brother. He said, "Chah! Allah, I will not do it. You know, Zirigu, I have a hot heart in my chest. How can I serve another man? Cook? Steward-boy? Garden-boy? Chah. It all means that some fool who is big only because he is white or because he can read book will make me a dog. I will beat him or kill him and go to prison before I am awake." He went to prison later because they say he did other things. But I don't know. I think he was a good man. He said to me: "You, you are a cool one. It would be better for you to do that than wandering. Go and train." I did. I worked in white men's homes for about two years. Setu's brother was not finding things easy. One day he said, "Zirigu, you are a sober man. You must think of marrying. You are already too old." I said, "Yes. Maybe I will go home next Christmas and marry." He said, "You know my sister, Setu?" "Yes," I said. "Her husband died. She has one child, a son. You are not a Believer and my father's ghost will curse me for what I'm going to ask you to do. But you are a good man and she is a good woman. Marry Setu and look after her for me." My young Master, I met and married Setu. Her brother was right. She is a good woman. Like most of our women, she always believes in a woman having her own little money, so that she does not have to go to her husband for everything. On the coast, she mostly sold roasted plantains and groundnuts. Here, she makes *kaffa*.

'And how did I come here, you are asking me, my young Master? I will tell you. The last white master I served on the coast liked me very much. When he was going to go away for good, he told me not go too far away from the bungalow. In fact, that I should stay in the boys' quarters for the first two months after he was gone. That in the third month, a new master would come from their country. My old master was going to leave a recommendation with me for the new master so that he would employ me. I said, "Yes, Master." But just a few days before he left, he let me know that there was a Government Rest House attached to his office in this area. That the keeper of it was going away for some reason of his own. My master knew it had a better salary. He had recommended me for it. That's how I came here.

'Yes, my Master, that is more than ten years ago. At first, it was only white people who came here. Then a few black men began coming too. Now, *they* don't come any more – I mean the white men. How can I be sorry? Do I sound sorry? Between me and you, I can say that I don't know whether it has made much difference for me or not. Sometimes I am really glad when I think that our own people have done so well. About two years after the white people left, I stopped wearing the uniform. No one seemed to notice. Now I can feel the type of person a visitor is and then I may or may not even wait at table. But that is all, I am still Zirigu. I thank God that my little sons here seem to be doing well at school. I don't think I will have money to send them to college. But I will not grieve about that. Setu is a good wife. For the rest, I don't know. I have lived here for many years. It is the only home the children know. I hope that by the time I am too old to be the keeper here, the children too will be old enough to look after themselves.

'Master, I'm sure it is very late. After all that *tuo* and now the *pito*, I'm sure you need a long night's sleep. I only hope you will not have to get up to look after running bowels.

'Sleep well, my young Master.'

'No, neither of us is going to bed yet. No, not until you have told me the rest of the story you promised.'

'Weyting?'

'You said you were going to tell me something else soon.'

'Hah, I don't know. But listen, my young Master, this place was not like this when I first came here. There was only one block to this main house with two rooms, A and B. With this front room here where we are sitting now. It was later, the first year or two after we had the freedom that they built C and D, and the other kitchen. It has never been used – I mean the other kitchen. If it had been built in the days of the white people, someone might have brought his own cook here with him some time to use it. But our people do not care about that kind of thing. And there has always been me. When they decided to build the other block, they gave notice that for about six months, people should not come and stay. At the same time, they decided the boys' quarters looked too bad and that it should be renovated. So Setu and I thought that we would go home for a while, leaving the children to stay here with some sisters of Setu's. We did not want their schooling to be interrupted. Yes, they said they were going to make the boys' quarters new. The place has always been sufficient for me. Not only because there is an extra room for the children to sleep in, but there is also that land with it. Every year, I have cultivated the plots and harvested good cassava, millet, okra and even yams. My young Master, much of the time, the four of us live on what we earn from this earth. And then we keep what Setu and I make from other work for more important things. Like buying the children's books, their uniforms and paying their fees. In the years the children were going to school free, we put by the money from those things for other necessary expenses. Because, my Master, for people like us, money is never, never idle. Sometimes Setu and I wonder how God created the other people who have so much money that they can put some in a bank. And yet, we also know that even we are better off than so many of our friends and relatives. But I should not burden you with the troubles of my whole clan. What I was saying is that this place seemed sufficient for us. But still, when they said they were going to do something about it I hoped they would put in a good lavatory, like the water-closet, and give us good lights. Electric lights. Yes, my Master, the lavatory in the boys' quarters is the old pail and have you not noticed we use kerosene lamps? So I thought, "Zirigu, now you can really become something. When the white people were here, and they were our masters, it was only understandable that they should have electric lights and water-closets and give us, the boys, latrine pails and kerosene lamps. But now we are independent they are going

to make this house new. My own people will give me a closet
and an electric light." I did not tell my thoughts to Setu
because I was afraid she would say that I wanted to have the
same things as my betters. And this is not good since Allah
wants us to be satisfied with our lot. She is a Moslem but I
am not a Moslem. You people think all of us from the north
are Moslems. It is because you do not know anything about
the north. Later, I knew from Setu herself that in spite of
Allah's wishes, she too had hoped for a water-closet and electric lights. But she had been afraid to discuss it with me
because she thought I would have laughed at her. I asked the
man who first told me about the work whether we could have
a water-closet and electric lights. He said he was in charge of
buying supplies and finding the people to come and do the
work. "Yes," he said, "that should not be difficult." He didn't
think it would add much to the cost of the work, especially as
they had already counted in the boys' quarters. But he would
have to discuss it with the real big men under whom he was
working. He was sure they would consider it a small matter
and even scold him for not going ahead with it without asking
them before. But still . . . And when we came, what did we
find? They had put fresh paint on the walls. They had re-
paired the steps leading to the rooms and they had made us a
little verandah. But there were no electric lights and in the
lavatory, no water-closet. I discovered they had taken away
the old pail and given me a new one. Ah, my Master, I did
not know I wanted these things so much until I knew I was
not going to get them. They had taken the old pail and given
me a new one. My own people who are big men do not think
I should use these good things they use. Something went out
of me then which has not returned since. I do not understand
why I was so pained and angry, but I was. Setu told me that
we deserved it for wanting to be like our betters. Allah had
punished us. But I do not agree with her. I do want not to
be like them . . . or like you. For over ten years, I had kept
this place well. I know I had, otherwise why did they still

28

keep me here? Being a keeper, cook-steward here is not a bad job. It is a good job, the type of small job which some big man would want to take and give to a poor and distant relative. And neither Setu nor I know any big men. So they have let us stay all these years because we kept the place well. I serve them well too. I do what they want. My hair is going grey. Is one or two electric bulbs too much to expect? At least, that would have meant not spending sixpences and shillings on kerosene. I have thought and thought and thought about it. I have never understood why. For a long time, I was drinking. I wanted to go away. I wanted to kill somebody. Any time I went to the office in town to get my pay and give my reports about the place, I felt like spitting into their eyes. Those scholars. But Setu talked to me. She said I was behaving like a child. That it is nothing. We should never forget who we are, that's all. Now the anger is gone, and I stay here. My young Master, what does "Independence" mean?'

In the Cutting of a Drink

I say, my uncles, if you are going to Accra and anyone tells you that the best place for you to drop down is at the Circle, then he has done you good, but . . . Hm . . . I even do not know how to describe it. . . .

'Are all these beings that are passing this way and that way human? Did men buy all these cars with money . . .?'

But my elders, I do not want to waste your time. I looked round and did not find my bag. I just fixed my eyes on the ground and walked on. . . . Do not ask me why. Each time I tried to raise my eyes, I was dizzy from the number of cars which were passing. And I could not stand still. If I did, I felt as if the whole world was made up of cars in motion. There is something somewhere, my uncles. Not desiring to deafen you with too long a story . . .

I stopped walking just before I stepped into the Circle itself. I stood there for a long time. Then a lorry came along and I beckoned to the driver to stop. Not that it really stopped.

'Where are you going?' he asked me.

'I am going to Mamprobi,' I replied. 'Jump in,' he said, and he started to drive away. Hm . . . I nearly fell down climbing in. As we went round the thing which was like a big bowl on a very huge stump of wood, I had it in mind to have a good look at it, and later Duayaw told me that it shoots water in the air . . . but the driver was talking to me, so I could not look at it properly. He told me he himself was not going to Ma-

mprobi but he was going to the station where I could take a
lorry which would be going there. . . .

Yes, my uncle, he did not deceive me. Immediately we
arrived at the station I found the driver of a lorry shouting
'Mamprobi, Mamprobi'. Finally when the clock struck about
two-thirty, I was knocking on the door of Duayaw. I did not
knock for long when the door opened. Ah, I say, he was fast
asleep, fast asleep I say, on a Saturday afternoon.

'How can folks find time to sleep on Saturday afternoons?'
I asked myself. We hailed each other heartily. My uncles,
Duayaw has done well for himself. His mother Nsedua is a
very lucky woman.

How is it some people are lucky with school and others are
not? Did not Mansa go to school with Duayaw here in this
very school which I can see for myself? What have we done
that Mansa should have wanted to stop going to school?

But I must continue with my tale. . . . Yes, Duayaw has
done well for himself. His room has fine furniture. Only it is
too small. I asked him why and he told me he was even lucky
to have got that narrow place that looks like a box. It is very
hard to find a place to sleep in the city. . . .

He asked me about the purpose of my journey. I told him
everything. How, as he himself knew, my sister Mansa had
refused to go to school after 'Klase Tri' and how my mother
had tried to persuade her to go . . .

My mother, do not interrupt me, everyone present here
knows you tried to do what you could by your daughter.

Yes, I told him how, after she had refused to go, we finally
took her to this woman who promised to teach her to keep
house and to work with the sewing machine . . . and how she
came home the first Christmas after the woman took her but
has never been home again, these twelve years.

Duayaw asked me whether it was my intention then to look
for my sister in the city. I told him yes. He laughed saying,
'You are funny. Do you think you can find a woman in this
place? You do not know where she is staying. You do not even

31

know whether she is married or not. Where can we find her
if someone big has married her and she is now living in one
of those big bungalows which are some ten miles from the
city?'

Do you cry 'My Lord', mother? You are surprised about
what I said about the marriage? Do not be. I was surprised
too, when he talked that way. I too cried 'My Lord' . . . Yes, I
too did, mother. But you and I have forgotten that Mansa
was born a girl and girls do not take much time to grow. We
are thinking of her as we last saw her when she was ten years
old. But mother, that is twelve years ago. . . .

Yes, Duayaw told me that she is by now old enough to
marry and to do something more than merely marry. I asked
him whether he knew where she was and if he knew whether
she had any children – 'Children?' he cried, and he started
laughing, a certain laugh. . . .

I was looking at him all the time he was talking. He told
me he was not just discouraging me but he wanted me to see
how big and difficult it was, what I proposed to do. I replied
that it did not matter. What was necessary was that even if
Mansa was dead, her ghost would know that we had not forgotten her entirely. That we had not let her wander in other
people's towns and that we had tried to bring her home. . . .

These are useless tears you have started to weep, my
mother. Have I said anything to show that she was dead?

Duayaw and I decided on the little things we would do the
following day as the beginning of our search. Then he gave me
water for my bath and brought me food. He sat by me while I
ate and asked me for news of home. I told him that his father
has married another woman and of how last year the *akatse*
spoiled all our cocoa. We know about that already. When I
finished eating, Duayaw asked me to stretch out my bones on
the bed and I did. I think I slept fine because when I opened
my eyes it was dark. He had switched on his light and there
was a woman in the room. He showed me her as a friend but I
think she is the girl he wants to marry against the wishes of

his people. She is as beautiful as sunrise, but she does not come from our parts. . . .

When Duayaw saw that I was properly awake, he told me it had struck eight o'clock in the evening and his friend had brought some food. The three of us ate together.

Do not say 'Ei', uncle, it seems as if people do this thing in the city. A woman prepares a meal for a man and eats it with him. Yes, they do so often.

My mouth could not manage the food. It was prepared from cassava and corn dough, but it was strange food all the same. I tried to do my best. After the meal, Duayaw told me we were going for a night out. It was then I remembered my bag. I told him that as matters stood, I could not change my cloth and I could not go out with them. He would not hear of it. 'It would certainly be a crime to come to this city and not go out on a Saturday night.' He warned me though that there might not be many people, or anybody at all, where we were going who would also be in cloth but I should not worry about that.

Cut me a drink, for my throat is very dry, my uncle. . . .

When we were on the street, I could not believe my eyes. The whole place was as clear as the sky. Some of these lights are very beautiful indeed. Everyone should see them . . . and there are so many of them! 'Who is paying for all these lights? I asked myself. I could not say that aloud for fear Duayaw would laugh.

We walked through many streets until we came to a big building where a band was playing. Duayaw went to buy tickets for the three of us.

You all know that I had not been to anywhere like that before. You must allow me to say that I was amazed. 'Ei, are all these people children of human beings? And where are they going? And what do they want?'

Before I went in, I thought the building was big, but when I went in, I realised the crowd in it was bigger. Some were in front of a counter buying drinks, others were dancing . . .

Yes, that was the case, uncle, we had gone to a place where they had given a dance, but I did not know.

Some people were sitting on iron chairs around iron tables. Duayaw told some people to bring us a table and chairs and they did. As soon as we sat down, Duayaw asked us what we would drink. As for me, I told him *lamlale* but his woman asked for 'Beer' . . .

Do not be surprised, uncles.

Yes, I remember very well, she asked for beer. It was not long before Duayaw brought them. I was too surprised to drink mine. I sat with my mouth open and watched the daughter of a woman cut beer like a man. The band had stopped playing for some time and soon they started again. Duayaw and his woman went to dance. I sat there and drank my *lamlale*. I cannot describe how they danced.

After some time, the band stopped playing and Duayaw and his woman came to sit down. I was feeling cold and I told Duayaw. He said, 'And this is no wonder, have you not been drinking this women's drink all the time?'

'Does it make one cold?' I asked him.

'Yes,' he replied. 'Did you not know that? You must drink beer.'

'Yes,' I replied. So he bought me beer. When I was drinking the beer, he told me I would be warm if I danced.

'You know I cannot dance the way you people dance,' I told him.

'And how do we dance?' he asked me.

'I think you all dance like white men and as I do not know how that is done, people would laugh at me,' I said. Duayaw started laughing. He could not contain himself. He laughed so much his woman asked him what it was all about. He said something in the white man's language and they started laughing again. Duayaw then told me that if people were dancing, they would be so busy that they would not have time to watch others dance. And also, in the city, no one cares if you dance well or not . . .

Yes, I danced too, my uncles. I did not know anyone, that is true. My uncle, do not say that instead of concerning myself with the business for which I had gone to the city, I went dancing. Oh, if you only knew what happened at this place, you would not be saying this. I would not like to stop somewhere and tell you the end . . . I would rather like to put a rod under the story, as it were, clear off every little creeper in the bush . . .

But as we were talking about the dancing, something made Duayaw turn to look behind him where four women were sitting by the table. . . . Oh! he turned his eyes quickly, screwed his face into something queer which I could not understand and told me that if I wanted to dance, I could ask one of those women to dance with me.

My uncles, I too was very surprised when I heard that. I asked Duayaw if people who did not know me would dance with me' He said 'Yes.' I lifted my eyes, my uncles, and looked at those four young women sitting round a table alone. They were sitting all alone, I say. I got up.

I hope I am making myself clear, my uncles, but I was trembling like water in a brass bowl.

Immediately one of them saw me, she jumped up and said something in that kind of white man's language which everyone, even those who have not gone to school, speak in the city. I shook my head. She said something else in the language of the people of the place. I shook my head again. Then I heard her ask me in Fante whether I wanted to dance with her. I replied 'Yes.'

Ei! my little sister, are you asking me a question? Oh! you want to know whether I found Mansa? I do not know. . . . Our uncles have asked me to tell everything that happened there, and you too! I am cooking the whole meal for you, why do you want to lick the ladle now?

Yes, I went to dance with her. I kept looking at her so much I think I was all the time stepping on her feet. I say, she was as black as you and I, but her hair was very long and fell

35

on her shoulders like that of a white woman. I did not touch it but I saw it was very soft. Her lips with that red paint looked like a fresh wound. There was no space between her skin and her dress. Yes, I danced with her. When the music ended, I went back to where I was sitting. I do not know what she told her companions about me, but I heard them laugh.

It was this time that something made me realise that they were all bad women of the city. Duayaw had told me I would feel warm if I danced, yet after I had danced, I was colder than before. You would think someone had poured water on me. I was unhappy thinking about these women. 'Have they no homes?' I asked myself. 'Do not their mothers like them? God, we are all toiling for our threepence to buy something to eat . . . but oh! God! this is no work.'

(When I thought of my own sister, who was lost, I became a little happy because I felt that although I had not found her, she was nevertheless married to a big man and all was well with her.)

When they started to play the band again, I went to the women's table to ask the one with whom I had danced to dance again. But someone had gone with her already. I got one of the two who were still sitting there. She went with me. When we were dancing she asked me whether it was true that I was a Fante. I replied 'Yes.' We did not speak again. When the band stopped playing, she told me to take her to where they sold things to buy her beer and cigarettes. I was wondering whether I had the money. When we were where the lights were shining brightly, something told me to look at her face. Something pulled at my heart.

'Young woman, is this the work you do?' I asked her.

'Young man, what work do you mean?' she too asked me. I laughed.

'Do you not know what work?' I asked again.

'And who are you to ask me such questions? I say, who are you? Let me tell you that any kind of work is work. You villager, you villager, who are you?' she screamed.

I was afraid. People around were looking at us. I laid my hands on her shoulders to calm her down and she hit them away.

'Mansa, Mansa,' I said. 'Do you not know me?' She looked at me for a long time and started laughing. She laughed, laughed as if the laughter did not come from her stomach. Yes, as if she was hungry.

'I think you are my brother,' she said. 'Hm.'

Oh, my mother and my aunt, oh, little sister, are you all weeping? As for you women!

What is there to weep about? I was sent to find a lost child. I found her a woman.

Cut me a drink . . .

Any kind of work is work. . . . This is what Mansa told me with a mouth that looked like clotted blood. Any kind of work is work . . . so do not weep. She will come home this Christmas.

My brother, cut me another drink. Any form of work is work . . . is work . . . is work!

The Message

'Look here my sister, it should not be said but they say they
opened her up.'
   'They opened her up?'
   'Yes, opened her up.'
   'And the baby removed?'
   'Yes, the baby removed.'
   'Yes, the baby removed.'
   'I say . . .'
   'They do not say, my sister.'
   'Have you heard it?'
   'What?'
   'This and this and that . . . '
   'A-a-ah! that is it . . .'
   '*Meewuo!*'
   'They don't say *meewuo* . . .'
   'And how is she?'
   'Am I not here with you? Do I know the highway which
leads to Cape Coast?'
   'Hmmm . . .'
   'And anyway how can she live? What is it like even giving
birth with a stomach which is whole . . . eh? . . . I am asking
you. And if you are always standing on the brink of death
who go to war with a stomach that is whole, then how would
she do whose stomach is open to the winds?'
   'Oh, *poo*, pity . . .'

38

'I say . . .'

My little bundle, come. You and I are going to Cape Coast today.

I am taking one of her own cloths with me, just in case. These people on the coast do not know how to do a thing and I am not going to have anybody mishandling my child's body. I hope they give it to me. Horrible things I have heard done to people's bodies. Cutting them up and using them for instructions. Whereas even murderers still have decent burials.

I see Mensima coming. . . . And there is Nkama too . . . and Adwoa Meenu. . . . Now they are coming to . . . '*poo* pity' me. Witches, witches, witches . . . they have picked mine up while theirs prosper around them, children, grandchildren and great-grandchildren – theirs shoot up like mushrooms.

'Esi, we have heard of your misfortune . . .'

'That our little lady's womb has been opened up . . .'

'And her baby removed . . .'

Thank you very much.

'Has she lived through it?'

I do not know.

'Esi, bring her here, back home whatever happens.'

Yoo, thank you. If the government's people allow it, I shall bring her home.

'And have you got ready your things?'

Yes. . . . No.

I cannot even think well.

It feels so noisy in my head. . . . Oh my little child. . . . I am wasting time. . . . And so I am going . . .

Yes, to Cape Coast.

No, I do not know anyone there now but do you think no one would show me the way to this big hospital . . . if I asked around?

Hmmm . . . it's me has ended up like this. I was thinking that everything was alright now. . . . *Yoo*. And thank you too. Shut the door for me when you are leaving. You may stay too long outside if you wait for me, so go home and be about your business. I will let you know when I bring her in.

'Maami Amfoa, where are you going?'

My daughter, I am going to Cape Coast.

'And what is our old mother going to do with such swift steps? Is it serious?'

My daughter, it is very serious.

'Mother, may God go with you.'

Yoo, my daughter.

'Eno, and what calls at this hour of the day?'

They want me in Cape Coast.

'Does my friend want to go and see how much the city has changed since we went there to meet the new Wesleyan Chairman, twenty years ago?'

My sister, do you think I have knees to go parading on the streets of Cape Coast?

'Is it heavy?'

Yes, very heavy indeed. They have opened up my grandchild at the hospital, *hi, hi, hi*. . . .

'Eno *due, due, due* . . . I did not know. May God go with you. . . .'

Thank you. *Yaa*.

'O, the world!'

'It's her grandchild. The only daughter of her only son. Do you remember Kojo Amisa who went to sodja and fell in the great war, overseas?'

'Yes, it's his daughter. . . .'

. . . O, *poo*, pity.

'Kobina, run to the street, tell Draba Anan to wait for Nana Amfoa.'

'. . . Draba Anan, Draba, my mother says I must come and tell you to wait for Nana Amfoa.'

'And where is she?'

'There she comes.'

'Just look at how she hops like a bird . . . does she think we are going to be here all day? And anyway we are full already . . .'

O, you drivers!

'What have drivers done?'

'And do you think it shows respect when you speak in this way? It is only that things have not gone right; but she could, at least have been your mother. . . .'

'But what have I said? I have not insulted her. I just think that only Youth must be permitted to see Cape Coast, the town of the Dear and Expensive. . . .'

'And do you think she is going on a peaceful journey? The only daughter of her only son has been opened up and her baby removed from her womb.'

O . . . God.

O

O

O

Poo, pity.

'Me . . . *poo* – pity, I am right about our modern wives I always say they are useless as compared with our mothers.

'You drivers!'

'Now what have your modern wives done?'

'Am I not right what I always say about them?'

'You go and watch them in the big towns. All so thin and dry as sticks – you can literally blow them away with your breath. No decent flesh anywhere. Wooden chairs groan when they meet with their hard exteriors.'

'O you drivers. . . .'

'But of course all drivers . . .'

'What have I done? Don't all my male passengers agree with me? These modern girls. . . . Now here is one who cannot even have a baby in a decent way. But must have the baby removed from her stomach. *Tchiaa!*'

'What . . .'

'Here is the old woman.'

'Whose grandchild . . .?'

'Yes.'

'Nana, I hear you are coming to Cape Coast with us.'

C

Yes my master.

'We nearly left you behind but we heard it was you and that it is a heavy journey you are making.'

Yes my master . . . thank you my master.

'Push up please . . . push up. Won't you push up? Why do you all sit looking at me with such eyes as if I was a block of wood?'

'It is not that there is nowhere to push up to. Five fat women should go on that seat, but look at you!

'And our own grandmother here is none too plump herself. . . . Nana, if they won't push, come to the front seat with me.'

'. . . *Hei*, scholar, go to the back. . . .

'. . . And do not scowl on me. I know your sort too well. Something tells me you do not have any job at all. As for that suit you are wearing and looking so grand in, you hired or borrowed it. . . .'

'Oh you drivers!'

Oh you drivers . . .

The scholar who read this tengram thing, said it was made about three days ago. My lady's husband sent it. . . . Three days. . . . God – that is too long ago. Have they buried her . . . where? Or did they cut her up. . . . I should not think about it . . . or something will happen to me. Eleven or twelve . . . Efua Panyin, Okuma, Kwame Gyasi and who else? But they should not have left me here. Sometimes . . . ah, I hate this nausea. But it is this smell of petrol. Now I have remembered I never could travel in a lorry. I always was so sick. But now I hope at least that will not happen. These young people will think it is because I am old and they will laugh. At least if I knew the child of my child was alive, it would have been good. And the little things she sent me. . . . Sometimes some people like Mensima and Nkansa make me feel as if I had been a barren woman instead of only one with whom infant-mortality pledged friendship . . .

I will give her that set of earrings, bracelet and chain which Odwumfo Ata made for me. It is the most beautiful and the

most expensive thing I have. . . . It does not hurt me to think
that I am going to die very soon and have them and their
children gloating over my things. After all what did they
swallow my children for? It does not hurt me at all. If I had
been someone else, I would have given them all away before
I died. But it does not matter. They can share their own curse.
Now, that is the end of me and my roots. . . . Eternal death
has worked like a warrior rat, with diabolical sense of duty, to
gnaw my bottom. Everything is finished now. The vacant lot
is swept and the scraps of old sugar-cane pulp, dry sticks and
bunches of hair burnt . . . how it reeks, the smoke!

'O, Nana do not weep . . .'

'Is the old woman weeping?'

'If the only child of your only child died, won't you
weep?'

'Why do you ask me? Did I know her grandchild is
dead?'

'Where have you been, not in this lorry? Where were your
ears when we were discussing it?'

'I do not go putting my mouth in other people's affairs . . .'

'So what?'

'So go and die.'

'*Hei, hei*, it is prohibited to quarrel in my lorry.'

'Draba, here is me, sitting quiet and this lady of muscles
and bones being cheeky to me.'

'Look, I can beat you.'

'Beat me . . . beat me . . . let's see.'

'*Hei*, you are not civilised, eh?'

'Keep quiet and let us think, both of you, or I will put
you down.'

'Nana, do not weep. There is God above.'

Thank you my master.

'But we are in Cape Coast already.'

Meewuo! My God, hold me tight or something will happen
to me.

My master, I will come down here.

'O Nana, I thought you said you were going to the hospital. . . . We are not there yet.'

I am saying maybe I will get down here and ask my way around.

'Nana, you do not know these people, eh? They are very impudent here. They have no use for old age. So they do not respect it. Sit down, I will take you there.'

Are you going there, my master?

'No, but I will take you there.'

Ah, my master, your old mother thanks you. Do not shed a tear when you hear of my death . . . my master, your old mother thanks you.

I hear there is somewhere where they keep corpses until their owners claim them . . . if she has been buried, then I must find her husband . . . Esi Amfoa, what did I come to do under this sky? I have buried all my children and now I am going to bury my only grandchild!

'Nana we are there.'

Is this the hospital?

'Yes, Nana. What is your child's name?'

Esi Amfoa. Her father named her after me.

'Do you know her European name?'

No, my master.

'What shall we do?'

'. . . *Ei* lady, Lady Nurse, we are looking for somebody.'

'You are looking for somebody and can you read? If you cannot, you must ask someone what the rules in the hospital are. You can only come and visit people at three o'clock.'

Lady, please. She was my only grandchild . . .

'Who? And anyway, it is none of our business.'

'Nana, you must be patient . . . and not cry . . .'

'Old woman, why are you crying, it is not allowed here. No one must make any noise . . .'

My lady, I am sorry but she was all I had.

'Who? Oh, are you the old woman who is looking for somebody?'

Yes.

'Who is he?'

She was my granddaughter – the only child of my only son.

'I mean, what was her name?'

Esi Amfoa.

'Esi Amfoa . . . Esi Amfoa. I am sorry, we do not have anyone whom they call like that here.'

Is that it?

'Nana, I told you they may know only her European name here.'

My master, what shall we do then?

'What is she ill with?'

She came here to have a child . . .

'. . . And they say, they opened her stomach and removed the baby.'

'Oh . . . oh, I see.'

My Lord, hold me tight so that nothing will happen to me now.

'I see. It is the Caesarean case.'

'Nurse, you know her?'

And when I take her back, Anona Ebusuafo will say that I did not wait for them to come with me . . .

'Yes. Are you her brother?'

'No. I am only the driver who brought the old woman.'

'Did she bring all her clan?'

'No. She came alone.'

'Strange thing for a villager to do.'

I hope they have not cut her up already.

'Did she bring a whole bag full of cassava and plantain and kenkey?'

'No. She has only her little bundle.'

'Follow me. But you must not make any noise. This is not the hour for coming here . . .'

My master, does she know her?

'Yes.'

I hear it is very cold where they put them . . .

. . . . .

It was feeding time for new babies. When old Esi Amfoa saw young Esi Amfoa, the latter was all neat and nice. White sheets and all. She did not see the beautiful stitches under the sheets. 'This woman is a tough bundle,' Dr. Gyamfi had declared after the identical twins had been removed, the last stitches had been threaded off and Mary Koomson, alias Esi Amfoa, had come to.

The old woman somersaulted into the room and lay groaning, not screaming, by the bed. For was not her last pot broken? So they lay them in state even in hospitals and not always cut them up for instruction?

The Nursing Sister was furious. Young Esi Amfoa spoke. And this time old Esi Amfoa wept loud and hard – wept all her tears.

Scrappy nurse-under-training, Jessy Treeson, second-generation-Cape-Coaster-her-grandmother-still-remembered-at-Egyaa No. 7 said, 'As for these villagers,' and giggled.

Draba Anan looked hard at Jessy Treeson, looked hard at her, all of her: her starched uniform, apron and cap . . . and then dismissed them all. . . . 'Such a cassava stick . . . but maybe I will break my toe if I kicked at her buttocks,' he thought.

And by the bed the old woman was trying hard to rise and look at the only pot which had refused to get broken.

Certain Winds from the South

M'ma Asana eyed the wretched pile of cola-nuts, spat, and picked up the reed-bowl. Then she put down the bowl, picked up one of the nuts, bit at it, threw it back, spat again, and stood up. First, a sharp little ache, just a sharp little one, shot up from somewhere under her left ear. Then her eyes became misty.

'I must check on those logs,' she thought, thinking this misting of her eyes was due to the chill in the air. She stooped over the nuts.

'You never know what evil eyes are prowling this dusk over these grasslands – I must pick them up quickly.'

On the way back to the kraal, her eyes fell on the especially patchy circles that marked where the old pits had been. At this time, in the old days, they would have been full to bursting and as one scratched out the remains of the out-going season, one felt a near-sexual thrill of pleasure looking at these pits, just as one imagines a man might feel who looks upon his wife in the ninth month of pregnancy.

Pregnancy and birth and death and pain; and death again. . . . When there are no more pregnancies, there are no more births and therefore, no more deaths. But there is only one death and only one pain . . .

Show me a fresh corpse my sister, so I can weep you old tears.

The pit of her belly went cold, then her womb moved and she had to lean by the doorway. In twenty years, Fuseni's has

been the only pregnancy and the only birth . . . twenty years,
and the first child and a male! In the old days, there would
have been bucks and you got scolded for serving a woman
in maternity a duicker. But these days, those mean poachers
on the government reserves sneak away their miserable
duickers, such wretched hinds! Yes, they sneak away even the
duickers to the houses of those sweet-toothed southerners.

In the old days, how time goes, and how quickly age comes.
But then does one expect to grow younger when one starts
getting grandchildren? Allah be praised for a grandson.

The fire was still strong when she returned to the room.
. . . M'ma Asana put the nuts down. She craned her neck into
the corner. At least those logs should take them to the following week. For the rest of the evening, she set about preparing
for the morrow's marketing.

The evening prayers were done. The money was in the
bag. The grassland was still, Hawa was sleeping and so was
Fuseni. M'ma came out to the main gate, first to check up if
all was well outside and then to draw the door across. It was
not the figure, but rather the soft rustle of light footsteps
trying to move still more lightly over the grass that caught her
attention.

'If only it could be my husband.'

But of course it was not her husband!

'Who comes?'

'It is me, M'ma.'

'You Issa, my son?'

'Yes, M'ma.'

'They are asleep.'

'I thought so. That is why I am coming now.'

There was a long pause in the conversation as they both
hesitated about whether the son-in-law should go in to see
Hawa and the baby or not. Nothing was said about this
struggle but then one does not say everything.

M'ma Asana did not see but she felt him win the battle.
She crossed the threshold outside and drew the door behind

her. Issa led the way. They did not walk far, however. They just turned into a corner between two of the projecting pillars in the wall of the kraal. It was Issa who stood with his back to the wall. And this was as it should have been, for it was he who needed the comforting coolness of it for his backbone.

'M'ma, is Fuseni well?'

'Yes.'

'M'ma, is Hawa well?'

'Yes.'

'M'ma please tell me, is Fuseni very well?'

'A-ah, my son. For what are you troubling yourself so much?' 'Fuseni is a new baby who was born not more than ten days. How can I tell you he is very well? When a grown-up goes to live in other people's village . . .'

'M'ma.'

'What is it?'

'No. Please it is nothing.'

'My son, I cannot understand you this evening. Yes, if you, a grown-up person, goes to live in another village, will you say after the first few days that you are perfectly well?'

'No.'

'Shall you not get yourself used to their food? Shall you not find first where you can get water for yourself and your sheep?'

'Yes, M'ma.'

'Then how is it you ask me if Fuseni is very well? The navel is healing very fast . . . and how would it not? Not a single navel of all that I have cut here got infected. Shall I now cut my grandson's and then sit and see it rot? But it is his male that I can't say. Mallam did it neat and proper and it must be alright. Your family is not noted for males that rot, is it now?'

'No, M'ma.'

'Then let your heart lie quiet in your breast. Fuseni is well but we cannot say how well yet.'

'I have heard you, M'ma . . . M'ma . . .'

49

'Yes, my son.'

'M'ma, I am going South.'

'Where did you say?'

'South.'

'How far?'

'As far as the sea. M'ma I thought you would understand.'

'Have I spoken yet?'

'No, you have not.'

'Then why did you say that?'

'That was not well said.'

'And what are you going to do there?'

'Find some work .'

'What work?'

'I do not know.'

'Yes, you know, you are going to cut grass.'

'Perhaps.'

'But my son, why must you travel that far just to cut grass? Is there not enough of it all round here? Around this kraal, your father's and all the others in the village? Why do you not cut these?'

'M'ma, you know it is not the same. If I did that here people will think I am mad. But over there, I have heard that not only do they like it but the government pays you to do it.'

'Even still, our men do not go South to cut grass. This is for those further north. They of the wilderness, it is they who go South to cut grass. This is not for our men.'

'Please M'ma, already time is going. Hawa is a new mother and Fuseni my first child.'

'And yet you are leaving them to go South and cut grass.'

'But M'ma, what will be the use in my staying here and watching them starve? You yourself know that all the cola went bad, and even if they had not, with trade as it is, how much money do you think I would have got from them? And that is why I am going. Trade is broken and since we do not know when things will be good again, I think it will be better for me to go away.'

'Does Hawa know?'

'No, she does not.'

'Are you coming to wake her up at this late hour to tell her?'

'No.'

'You are wise.'

'M'ma, I have left everything in the hands of Amadu. He will come and see Hawa tomorrow.'

'Good. When shall we expect you back?'

'. . .'

'Issa . . .'

'M'ma.'

'When shall we expect you back?'

'M'ma, I do not know. Perhaps next Ramaddan.'

'Good.'

'So I go now.'

'Allah go with you.'

'And may His prophet look after you all.'

M'ma went straight back to bed, but not to sleep. And how could she sleep? At dawn, her eyes were still wide-open.

'Is his family noted for males that rot? No, certainly not. It is us who are noted for our unlucky females. There must be something wrong with them. . . . Or how is it we cannot hold our men? Allah, how is it?

Twenty years ago. Twenty years, perhaps more than twenty years . . . perhaps more than twenty years and Allah please, give me strength to tell Hawa.

Or shall I go to the market now and then tell her when I come back? No. Hawa, Hawa, now look at how you are stretched down there like a log! Does a mother sleep like this? Hawa, H-a-a-w-a! Oh, I shall not leave you alone. . . . And how can you hear your baby when it cries in the night since you die when you sleep?

. . . Listen to her asking me questions! Yes, it is broad daylight. I thought you really were dead. If it is cold, draw your blanket round you and listen to me for I have something to tell you.

Hawa, Issa has gone South.

And why do you stare at me with such shining eyes? I am telling you that Issa is gone south.

And what question do you think you are asking me? How could he take you along when you have a baby whose navel wound has not even healed yet?

He went away last night.

Don't ask me why I did not come to wake you up. What should I have woken you up for?

Listen, Issa said he could not stay here and just watch you and Fuseni starve.

He is going South to find work and . . . Hawa, where do you think you are getting up to go to? Issa is not at the door waiting for you. The whole neighbourhood is not up yet, so do not let me shout . . . and why are you behaving like a baby? Now you are a mother and you must decide to grow up . . . where are you getting up to go? Listen to me telling you this. Issa is gone. He went last night because he wants to catch the government bus that leaves Tamale very early in the morning. So . . .

Hawa, ah-ah, are you crying? Why are you crying? That your husband has left you to go and work? Go on weeping, for he will bring the money to look after me and not you. . . . I do not understand, you say? May be I do not. . . . See, now you have woken up Fuseni. Sit down and feed him and listen to me . . .

Listen to me and I will tell you of another man who left his newborn child and went away.

Did he come back? No, he did not come back. But do not ask me any more questions for I will tell you all.

He used to go and come, then one day he went away and never came back. Not that he had had to go like the rest of them . . .

Oh, they were soldiers. I am talking of a soldier. He need

not have gone to be a soldier. After all, his father was one of the richest men of this land. He was not the eldest son, that is true, but still, there were so many things he could have done to look after himself and his wife when he came to marry. But he would not listen to anybody. How could he sit by and have other boys out-do him in smartness?

Their clothes that shone and shone with pressing. . . . I say, you could have looked into any of them and put khole under your eyes. And their shoes, how they roared! You know soldiers for yourself. Oh, the stir on the land when they came in from the South! Mothers spoke hard and long to daughters about the excellencies of proper marriages, while fathers hurried through with betrothals. Most of them were afraid of getting a case like that of Memunat on their hands. Her father had taken the cattle and everything and then Memunat goes and plays with a soldier. Oh, the scandal she caused herself then!

Who was this Memunat? No, she is not your friend's mother. No, this Memunat in the end ran away South herself. We hear she became a bad woman in the city and made a lot of money. No, we do not hear of her now – she is not dead either, for we hear such women usually go to their homes to die, and she has not come back here yet.

But us, we were different. I had not been betrothed.

Do you ask me why I say we? Because this man was your father. . . . Ah-ah, you open your mouth and eyes wide? Yes my child, it is of your father I am speaking.

No, I was not lying when I told you that he died. But keep quiet and listen. . . .

He was going South to get himself a house for married soldiers.

No, it was not that time he did not come back. He came here, but not to fetch me.

He asked us if we had heard of the war.

Had we not heard of the war? Was it not difficult to get things like tinned fish, kerosene and cloth?

Yes, we said, but we thought it was only because the traders were not bringing them in.

Well yes, he said, but the traders do not get them even in the South.

And why, we asked.

O you people, have you not heard of the German-people? He had no patience with us. He told us that in the South they were singing dirty songs with their name.

But when are we going, I asked him.

What he told me was that that was why he had come. He could not take me along with him. You see, he said, since we were under the Anglis-people's rule and they were fighting with the German-people . . .

Ask me, my child, for that was exactly what I asked him, what has all that got to do with you and me? Why can I not come South with you?

Because I have to travel to the lands beyond the sea and fight . . .

In other people's war? My child, it is as if you were there. That is what I asked him.

But it is not as simple as that, he said.

We could not understand him. You shall not go, said his father. You shall not go, for it is not us fighting with the Grunshies or the Gonjas. . . . I know about the Anglis-people but not about any German-people, but anyway they are in their land.

Of course his father was playing, and so was I.

A soldier must obey at all time, he said.

I wanted to give him so many things to take with him but he said he could only take cola.

Then the news came. It did not enter my head, for there all was empty. Everything went into my womb. You were just three days old.

The news was like fire which settled in the pit of my belly. And from time to time, some would shoot up, searing my womb, singeing my intestines and burning up and up and up until I screamed with madness when it got into my head.

I had told myself when you were born that it did not matter you were a girl, all gifts from Allah are good and anyway he was coming back and we were going to have many more children, lots of sons.

But Hawa, you had a lot of strength, for how you managed to live I do not know. Three days you were and suddenly like a rivulet that is hit by an early harmattan, my breasts went dry. . . . Hawa, you have a lot of strength.

Later, they told me that if I could go South and prove to the government's people that I was his wife, I would get a lot of money.

But I did not go. It was him I wanted, not his body turned into gold.

I never saw the South.

Do you say oh? My child I am always telling you that the world was created a long while ago and it is old-age one has not seen but not youth. So do not say oh.

Those people, the government's people, who come and go, tell us trade is bad now, and once again there is no tinned fish and no cloth. But this time they say, this is because our children are going to get them in abundance one day.

Issa has gone South now because he cannot afford even goat flesh for his wife in maternity. This has to be, so that Fuseni can stay with his wife and eat cow-meat with her? Hmm. And he will come back alive . . . perhaps not next Ramaddan but the next. Now, my daughter, you know of another man who went to fight. And he went to fight in other people's war and he never came back.

I am going to the market now. Get up early to wash Fuseni. I hope to get something for those miserable colas. There is enough rice to make *tuo*, is there not? Good. Today even if it takes all the money, I hope to get us some smoked fish, the biggest I can find, to make us a real good sauce. . . .'

No Sweetness Here

He was beautiful, but that was not important. Beauty does not play such a vital role in a man's life as it does in a woman's, or so people think. If a man's beauty is so ill-mannered as to be noticeable, people discreetly ignore its existence. Only an immodest girl like me would dare comment on a boy's beauty. 'Kwesi is so handsome,' I was always telling his mother. 'If ever I am transferred from this place, I will kidnap him.' I enjoyed teasing the dear woman and she enjoyed being teased about him. She would look scandalised, pleased and alarmed all in one fleeting moment.

'Ei, Chicha. You should not say such things. The boy is not very handsome really.' But she knew she was lying. 'Besides, Chicha, who cares whether a boy is handsome or not?' Again she knew that at least she cared, for, after all, didn't the boy's wonderful personality throw a warm light on the mother's lively though already waning beauty? Then gingerly, but in a remarkably matter-of-fact tone, she would voice out her gnawing fear. 'Please Chicha, I always know you are just making fun of me, but please, promise me you won't take Kwesi away with you.' Almost at once her tiny mouth would quiver and she would hide her eyes in her cloth as if ashamed of her great love and her fears. But I understood. 'O, Maami, don't cry, you know I don't mean it.'

'Chicha I am sorry, and I trust you. Only I can't help fearing, can I? What will I do, Chicha, what would I do, should something happen to my child?' She would raise her pretty eyes, glistening with unshed tears.

'Nothing will happen to him,' I would assure her. 'He is a good boy. He does not fight and therefore there is no chance of anyone beating him. He is not dull, at least not too dull, which means he does not get more cane-lashes than the rest of his mates. . . .'

'Chicha, I shall willingly submit to your canes if he gets his sums wrong,' she would hastily intervene.

'Don't be funny. A little warming-up on a cold morning wouldn't do him any harm. But if you say so, I won't object to hitting that soft flesh of yours.' At this, the tension would break and both of us begin laughing. Yet I always went away with the image of her quivering mouth and unshed tears in my mind.

Maami Ama loved her son; and this is a silly statement, as silly as saying Maami Ama is a woman. Which mother would not? At the time of this story, he had just turned ten years old. He was in Primary Class Four and quite tall for his age. His skin was as smooth as shea-butter and as dark as charcoal. His black hair was as soft as his mother's. His eyes were of the kind that always remind one of a long dream on a hot afternoon. It is indecent to dwell on a boy's physical appearance, but then Kwesi's beauty was indecent.

The evening was not yet come. My watch read 4.15 p.m., that ambiguous time of the day which these people, despite their great ancient astronomic knowledge, have always failed to identify. For the very young and very old, it is certainly evening, for they've stayed at home all day and they begin to persuade themselves that the day is ending. Bored with their own company, they sprawl in the market-place or by their own walls. The children begin to whimper for their mothers, for they are tired with playing 'house'. Fancying themselves starving, they go back to what was left of their lunch, but really they only pray that mother will come home from the farm soon. The very old certainly do not go back on lunch remains but they do bite back at old conversational topics which were fresh at ten o'clock.

'I say, Kwame, as I was saying this morning, my first wife was a most beautiful woman,' old Kofi would say.

'Oh! yes, yes, she was an unusually beautiful girl. I remember her.' Old Kwame would nod his head but the truth was he was tired of the story and he was sleepy. 'It's high time the young people came back from the farm.'

But I was a teacher, and I went the white man's way. School was over. Maami Ama's hut was at one end of the village and the school was at the other. Nevertheless it was not a long walk from the school to her place because Bamso is not really a big village. I had left my books to little Grace Ason to take home for me; so I had only my little clock in my hand and I was walking in a leisurely way. (As I passed the old people, they shouted their greetings. It was always the Fanticised form of the English.)

'Kudiimin-o, Chicha.' Then I would answer, 'Kudiimin, Nana.' When I greeted first, the response was 'Tanchiw'.

'Chicha, how are you?'

'Nana, I am well.'

'And how are the children?'

'Nana, they are well.'

'*Yoo*, that is good.' When an old man felt inclined to be talkative, especially if he had more than me for audience, he would compliment me on the work I was doing. Then he would go on to the assets of education, especially female education, ending up with quoting Dr. Aggrey.

So this evening too, I was delayed: but it was as well, for when I arrived at the hut, Maami Ama had just arrived from the farm. The door opened, facing the village, and so I could see her. Oh, that picture is still vivid in my mind. She was sitting on a low stool with her load before her. Like all the loads the other women would bring from the farms into their homes, it was colourful with miscellaneous articles. At the very bottom of the wide wooden tray were the cassava and yam tubers, rich muddy brown, the colour of the earth. Next were the plantain, of the green colour of the woods from which they came. Then there were the gay vegetables, the scarlet pepper, garden eggs, golden pawpaw and crimson tomatoes. Over this riot of colours the little woman's eyes were fixed, absorbed, while the tiny hands delicately picked the pepper. I made a scratchy noise at the door. She looked up and smiled. Her smile was a wonderful flashing whiteness.

'Oh Chicha, I have just arrived.'

'So I see. *Ayekoo.*'

'*Yaa*, my own. And how are you, my child?'

'Very well, Mother. And you?'

'Tanchiw. Do sit down, there's a stool in that corner. Sit down. Mmmm. . . . Life is a battle. What can we do? We are just trying, my daughter.'

'Why were you longer at the farm today?'

'After weeding that plot I told you about last week, I thought I would go for one or two yams.'

'Ah!' I cried.

'You know tomorrow is Ahobaa. Even if one does not feel happy, one must have some yam for old Ahor.'

'Yes. So I understand. The old saviour deserves it. After all it is not often that a man offers himself as a sacrifice to the gods to save his people from a pestilence.'

'No, Chicha, we were so lucky.'

'But Maami Ama, why do you look so sad? After all, the yams are quite big.' She gave me a small grin, looking at the yams she had now packed at the corner.

'Do you think so? Well, they are the best of the lot. My daughter, when life fails you, it fails you totally. One's yams reflect the total sum of one's life. And mine look wretched enough.'

'O, Maami, why are you always speaking in this way? Look at Kwesi, how many mothers can boast of such a son? Even though he is only one, consider those who have none at all. Perhaps some woman is sitting at some corner envying you '

She chuckled. 'What an unhappy woman she must be who would envy Ama! But thank you, I should be grateful for Kwesi.'

After that we were quiet for a while. I always loved to see her moving quietly about her work. Having finished unpacking, she knocked the dirt out of the tray and started making fire to prepare the evening meal. She started humming a religious lyric. She was a Methodist.

We are fighting
We are fighting
We are fighting for Canaan, the Heavenly Kingdom above.

I watched her and my eyes became misty, she looked so much like my own mother. Presently, the fire began to smoke. She turned round. 'Chicha.'

'Maami Ama.'

'Do you know that tomorrow I am going to have a formal divorce?'

'Oh!' And I could not help the dismay in my voice.

I had heard, soon after my arrival in the village, that the parents of that most beautiful boy were as good as divorced. I had hoped they would come to a respectful understanding for the boy's sake. Later on when I got to know his mother, I had wished for this, for her own sweet self's sake too. But as time went on I had realised this could not be or was not even desirable. Kodjo Fi was a selfish and bullying man, whom no decent woman ought to have married. He got on marvellously with his two other wives but they were three of a feather. Yet I was sorry to hear Maami was going to have a final breach with him.

'Yes, I am,' she went on. 'I should. What am I going on like this for? What is man struggling after? Seven years is a long time to bear ill-usage from a man coupled with contempt and insults from his wives. What have I done to deserve the abuse of his sisters? And his mother!'

'Does she insult you too?' I exclaimed.

'Why not? Don't you think she would? Considering that I don't buy her the most expensive cloths on the market and I don't give her the best fish from my soup, like her daughters-in-law do.'

I laughed. 'The mean old witch!'

'Chicha, don't laugh. I am quite sure she wanted to eat Kwesi but I baptised him and she couldn't.'

'Oh, don't say that, Maami. I am quite sure they all like you, only you don't know.'

'My child, they don't. They hate me.'

But what happened?' I asked the question I had wanted to ask for so long.

'You would ask, Chicha! I don't know. They suddenly began hating me when Kwesi was barely two. Kodjo Fi reduced my housekeeping money and sometimes he refused to give me anything at all. He wouldn't eat my food. At first, I used to ask him why. He always replied, "It is nothing." If I had not been such an unlucky woman, his mother and sisters might have taken my side, but for me there was no one. That planting time, although I was his first wife, he allotted to me the smallest, thorniest plot.'

'Ei, what did you say about it?'

'What could I say? At that time my mother was alive, though my father was already dead. When I complained to her about the treatment I was getting from my husband, she told me that in marriage, a woman must sometimes be a fool. But I have been a fool for far too long a time.'

'Oh!' I frowned.

'Mother has died and left me and I was an only child too. My aunts are very busy looking after the affairs of their own daughters. I've told my uncles several times but they never take me seriously. They feel I am only a discontented woman.'

'You?' I asked in surprise.

'Perhaps you would not think so. But there are several who do feel like that in this village.'

She paused for a while, while she stared at the floor.

'You don't know, but I've been the topic of gossip for many years. Now, I only want to live on my own looking after my child. I don't think I will ever get any more children. Chicha, our people say a bad marriage kills the soul. Mine is fit for burial.'

'Maami, don't grieve.'

'My daughter, my mother and father who brought me to this world have left me alone and I've stopped grieving for them. When death summoned them, they were glad to lay down their tools and go to their parents. Yes, they loved me all right but even they had to leave me. Why should I make myself unhappy about a man for whom I ceased to exist a long time ago?'

She went to the big basket, took out some cassava and plantain, and sitting down began peeling them. Remembering she had forgotten the wooden bowl into which she would put the food, she got up to go for it.

'In this case,' I continued the conversation, 'what will happen to Kwesi?'

'What will happen to him?' she asked in surprise. 'This is no problem. They may tell me to give him to his father.'

'And would you?'

'No, I wouldn't.'

'And would you succeed in keeping him if his father insisted?'

'Well, I would struggle, for my son is his father's child but he belongs to my family.'

I sat there listening to these references to the age-old customs of which I had been ignorant. I was surprised. She washed the food, now cut into lumps, and arranged it in the cooking-pot. She added water and put it on the fire. She blew at it and it burst into flames.

'Maami Ama, has not your husband got a right to take Kwesi from you?' I asked her.

'He has, I suppose, but not entirely. Anyway, if the elders

who would make the divorce settlement ask me to let him go and stay with his father, I wouldn't refuse.'

'You are a brave woman.'

'Life has taught me to be brave,' she said, looking at me and smiling, 'By the way, what is the time?'

I told her, 'It is six minutes to six o'clock.'

'And Kwesi has not yet come home?' she exclaimed.

'Mama, here I am,' a piping voice announced.

'My husband, my brother, my father, my all-in-all, where are you?' And there he was. All at once, for the care-worn village woman, the sun might well have been rising from the east instead of setting behind the coconut palms. Her eyes shone. Kwesi saluted me and then his mother. He was a little shy of me and he ran away to the inner chamber. There was a thud which meant he had thrown his books down.

'Kwesi,' his mother called out to him. 'I have always told you to put your books down gently. I did not buy them with sand, and you ought to be careful with them.'

He returned to where we were. I looked at him. He was very dirty. There was sand in his hair, ears and eyes. His uniform was smeared with mud, crayon and berry-juice. His braces were hanging down on one side. His mother gave an affectionate frown. 'Kwesi, you are very dirty, just look at yourself. You are a disgrace to me. Anyone would think your mother does not look after you well.' I was very much amused, for I knew she meant this for my ears. Kwesi just stood there, without a care in the world.

'Can't you play without putting sand in your hair?' his mother persisted.

'I am hungry,' he announced. I laughed.

'Shame, shame, and your chicha is here. Chicha, you see? He does not fetch me water. He does not fetch me firewood. He does not weed my farm on Saturdays as other schoolboys do for their mothers. He only eats and eats.' I looked at him; he fled again into the inner chamber for shame. We both started laughing at him. After a time I got up to go.

'Chicha, I would have liked you to eat before you went away; that's why I am hurrying up with the food.' Maami tried to detain me.

'Oh, it does not matter. You know I eat here when I come, but today I must go away. I have the children's books to mark.'

'Then I must not keep you away from your work.'

'Tomorrow I will come to see you,' I promised.

'*Yoo*, thank you.'

'Sleep well, Maami.'

'Sleep well, my daughter.' I stepped into the open air. The sun was far receding. I walked slowly away. Just before I was out of earshot, Maami shouted after me, 'And remember, if Kwesi gets his sums wrong, I will come to school to receive his lashes, if only you would tell me.'

'*Yoo*,' I shouted back. Then I went away.

The next day was Ahobaada. It was a day of rejoicing for everyone. In the morning, old family quarrels were being patched up. In Maami Ama's family all became peaceful. Her aunts had – or thought they had – reconciled themselves to the fact that, when Maami Ama's mother was dying, she had instructed her sisters, much to their chagrin, to give all her jewels to her only child. This had been one of the reasons why the aunts and cousins had left Ama so much to her own devices. After all, she has her mother's goods, what else does she need?' they were often saying. However, today, aunts, cousins and nieces have come to a better understanding. Ahobaa is a season of goodwill! Nevertheless, Ama is going to have a formal divorce today. . . .

It had not been laid down anywhere in the Education Ordinance that schoolchildren were to be given holidays during local festivals. And so no matter how much I sympathised with the kids, I could not give them a holiday, although Ahobaa was such an important occasion for them; they naturally felt it a grievance to be forced to go to school while their friends at home were eating so much yam and meat. But they had their revenge on me. They fidgeted the whole day. What was worse, the schoolroom was actually just one big shed. When I left the Class One chicks to look at the older ones, they chattered; when I turned to them, Class Two and Class Three began shouting. Oh, it was a fine situation. In the afternoon, after having gone home to taste some of the festival dishes, they nearly drove me mad. So I was relieved when it was three o'clock. Feeling no sense of guilt, I turned them all out to play. They rushed out to the field. I packed my books on the table for little Grace to take home. My intention was to go and see the divorce proceedings which had begun at one o'clock and then come back at four to dismiss them. These divorce cases took hours to settle, and I hoped I would hear some of it.

As I walked down between the rows of desks, I hit my leg against one. The books on it tumbled down. As I picked them up I saw they belonged to Kwesi. It was the desk he shared with a little girl. I began thinking about him and the unhappy connection he had with what was going on at that moment down in the village. I remembered every word of the conversation I had had with his mother the previous evening. I became sad at the prospect of a possible separation from the mother who loved him so much and whom he loved. From his infancy they had known only each other, a lonely mother and a lonely son. Through the hot sun, she had carried him on her back as she weeded her cornfield. How could she dare to put him down under a tree in the shade when there was no one to look after him? Other women had their own younger sisters or those of their husbands to help with the baby; but she had had no one. The only face the little one had known was his mother's. And now . . .

'But,' I told myself, 'I am sure it will be all right with him.'
'Will it?' I asked myself.
'Why not? He is a happy child.'
'Does that solve the problem?'
'Not altogether, but . . .'

'No buts; one should think of the house into which he would be taken now. He may not be a favourite there.'

But my other voice told me that a child need not be a favourite to be happy.

I had to bring the one-man argument to an end. I had to hurry. Passing by the field, I saw some of the boys playing football. At the goal at the further end was a headful of hair shining in the afternoon sun. I knew the body to which it belonged. A goalkeeper is a dubious character in infant soccer. He is either a good goalkeeper and that is why he is at the goal, which is usually difficult to know in a child, or he is a bad player. If he is a bad player, he might as well be in the goal as anywhere else. Kwesi loved football, that was certain, and he was always the goalkeeper. Whether he was good or not I had never been able to see. Just as I passed, he caught a ball and his team clapped. I heard him give the little squeaky noise that passed for his laugh. No doubt he was a happy child.

Now I really ran into the village. I immediately made my way to Nana Kum's house, for the case was going on there. There was a great crowd in front of the house. Why were there so many people about? Then I remembered that it being a holiday, everyone was at home. And of course, after the eating and the drinking of palm-wine in the morning and midday, divorce proceedings certainly provide an agreeable diversion, especially when other people are involved and not ourselves.

The courtyard was a long one and as I jostled to where Maami Ama was sitting, pieces of comments floated into my ears. 'The elders certainly have settled the case fairly,' someone was saying. 'But it seemed as if Kodjo Fi had no strong proofs for his arguments,' another was saying. 'Well, they both have been sensible. If one feels one can't live with a woman, one might as well divorce her. And I hate a woman who cringes to a man,' a third said. Finally I reached her side. Around her were her family, her two aunts, Esi and Ama, her two cousins and the two uncles. To the right were the elders who were judging the case; opposite were Kodjo Fi and his family.

'I have come, Maami Ama,' I announced myself.

She looked at me. 'You ought to have been here earlier, the case has been settled already.'

'And how are things?' I inquired.

'I am a divorced woman.'

'What were his grounds for wanting to divorce you?'

'He said I had done nothing, he only wanted to . . .'

'Eh! Only the two of you know what went wrong,' the younger aunt cried out, reproachfully. 'If after his saying that, you had refused to be divorced, he would have had to pay the Ejecting Fee, but now he has got the better of you.'

'But aunt,' Maami protested, 'how could I refuse to be divorced?'

'It's up to you. I know it's your own affair, only I wouldn't like your mother's ghost to think that we haven't looked after you well.'

'I agree with you,' the elder aunt said.

'Maami Ama, what was your debt?' I asked her.

'It is quite a big sum.'

'I hope you too had something to reckon against him?'

'I did. He reckoned the dowry, the ten cloths he gave me, the Knocking Fee. . . .'

All this had been heard by Kodjo Fi and his family and soon they made us aware of it.

'Kodjo,' his youngest sister burst out, 'you forgot to reckon the Knife Fee.'

'No. *Yaa*, I did not forget,' Kodjo Fi told her. 'She had no brothers to whom I would give the fee.'

'It's all right then,' his second sister added.

But the rest of his womenfolk took this to be a signal for more free comments.

'She is a bad woman and I think you are well rid of her,' one aunt screamed.

'I think she is a witch,' the youngest sister said.

'Oh, that she is. Anyway, only witches have no brothers or sisters. They eat them in the mother's womb long before they are born.'

Ama's aunts and cousins had said nothing so far. They were inclined to believe Ama was a witch too. But Maami sat still. When the comments had gone down a bit, she resumed the conversation with me.

'As I was saying, Chicha, he also reckoned the price of the trunk he had given me and all the cost of the medicine he gave me to make me have more children. There was only the Cooking Cost for me to reckon against his.'

'Have you got money to pay the debt?' I asked her.

'No, but I am not going to pay it. My uncles will pay it out of the family fund and put the debt down against my name.'

'Oh!'

'But you are a fool,' Maami Ama's eldest aunt shouted at her.

'I say you are a fool,' she insisted.

'But aunt . . .' Maami Ama began to protest.

'Yes! And I hope you are not going to answer back. I was born before your mother and now that she is dead, I'm your mother! Besides, when she was alive I could scold her when she went wrong, and now I say you are a fool. For seven years you have struggled to look after a child. Whether he ate or not was your affair alone. Whether he had any cloth or not did not concern any other person. When Kwesi was a child he had no father. When he nearly died of measles, no grandmother looked in. As for aunts, he began getting them when he started going to school. And now you are allowing them to take him away from you. Now that he is grown enough to be counted among the living, a father knows he has got a son.'

'So, so!' Kodjo Fi's mother sneered at her. 'What did you think? That Kodjo would give his son as a present to you, eh? The boy belongs to his family, but he must be of some service to his father too.'

'Have I called your name?' Ama's aunt asked the old woman.

'You have not called her name but you were speaking against her son.' This again was from Kodjo Fi's youngest sister.

'And who are you to answer my mother back?' Ama's two cousins demanded of her.

'Go away. But who are you people?'

'Go away, too, you greedy lot.'

'It is you who are greedy, witches.'

'You are always calling other people witches. Only a witch can know a witch.'

Soon everyone was shouting at everyone else. The people who had come started going home, and only the most curious ones stood by to listen. Maami Ama was murmuring something under her breath which I could not hear. I persuaded her to come with me. All that time no word had passed between her and her ex-husband. As we turned to go, Kodjo Fi's mother shouted at her, 'You are hurt. But that is what you deserve. We will get the child. We will! What did you want to do with him?'

Maami Ama turned round to look at her. 'What are you putting yourself to so much trouble for? When Nana Kum said the boy ought to go and stay with his father, did I make any objection? He is at the school. Go and fetch him. Tomorrow, you can send your carriers to come and fetch his belongings from my hut.' These words were said quietly.

Then I remembered suddenly that I had to hurry to school to dismiss the children. I told Maami Ama to go home but that I would try to see her before night.

This time I did not go by the main street. I took the back door through back streets and lanes. It was past four already. As I hurried along, I heard a loud roaring sound which I took to be echoes of the quarrel, so I went my way. When I reached the school, I did not like what I saw. There was not a single childish soul anywhere. But everyone's books were there. The shed was as untidy as ever. Little Grace had left my books too.

Of course I was more than puzzled. 'How naughty these children are. How did they dare to disobey me when I had told them to wait here until I came to dismiss them?' It was no use looking around the place. They were not there. 'They need discipline,' I threatened to the empty shed. I picked up my books and clock. Then I noticed that Kwesi's desk was clean of all his books. Nothing need be queer about this; he had probably taken his home. As I was descending the hill the second time that afternoon, I saw that the whole school was at the other end of the main street. What were the children doing so near Maami Ama's place? I ran towards them.

I was not prepared for what I saw. As if intentionally, the children had formed a circle. When some of them saw me, they all began to tell me what had happened. But I did not hear a word. In the middle of the circle, Kwesi was lying flat on his back. His shirt was off. His right arm was swollen to the size of his head. I simply stood there with my mouth open. From the back yard, Maami Ama screamed, 'I am drowning, people of Bamso, come and save me!' Soon the whole village was there.

What is the matter? What has happened? Kwesi has been bitten by a snake. Where? Where? At school. He was playing football. Where? What has happened? Bitten by a snake, a snake, a snake.

Questions and answers were tossed from mouth to mouth in the shocked evening air. Meanwhile, those who knew about snake-bites were giving the names of different cures. Kwesi's father was looking anxiously at his son. That strong powerful man was almost stupid with shock and alarm. Dose upon dose was forced down the reluctant throat but nothing seemed to have any effect. Women paced up and down around the hut, totally oblivious of the fact that they had left their festival meals half prepared. Each one was trying to imagine how she would have felt if Kwesi had been her child, and in imagination they suffered more than the suffering mother. 'The gods and spirits of our fathers protect us from calamity!'

70

After what seemed an unbearably long time, the messenger who had been earlier sent to Surdo, the village next to Bamso, to summon the chief medicine man arrived, followed by the eminent doctor himself. He was renowned for his cure of snake-bites. When he appeared, everyone gave a sigh of relief. They all remembered someone, perhaps a father, brother or husband, he had snatched from the jaws of death. When he gave his potion to the boy, he would be violently sick, and then of course, he would be out of danger. The potion was given. Thirty minutes; an hour; two hours; three, four hours. He had not retched. Before midnight, he was dead. No grown-up in Bamso village slept that night. Kwesi was the first boy to have died since the school was inaugurated some six years previously. 'And he was his mother's only child. She has no one now. We do not understand it. Life is not sweet!' Thus ran the verdict.

The morning was very beautiful. It seemed as if every natural object in and around the village had kept vigil too. So they too were tired. I was tired too. I had gone to bed at about five o'clock in the morning and since it was a Saturday I could have a long sleep. At ten o'clock, I was suddenly roused from sleep by shouting. I opened my window but I could not see the speakers. Presently Kweku Sam, one of the young men in the village, came past my window. 'Good morning, Chicha.' He shouted his greeting to me.

'Good morning, Kweku,' I responded. 'What is the shouting about?'

'They are quarrelling.'

'And what are they quarrelling about now?'

'Each is accusing the other of having been responsible for the boy's death.'

'How?'

'Chicha, I don't know. Only women make too much trouble for themselves. It seems as if they are never content to sit quiet but they must always hurl abuse at each other. What has happened is too serious to be a subject for quarrels. Perhaps

71

the village has displeased the gods in some unknown way and that is why they have taken away this boy.' He sighed. I could not say anything to that. I could not explain it myself, and if the villagers believed there was something more in Kwesi's death than the ordinary human mind could explain, who was I to argue?

'Is Maami Ama herself there?'

'No, I have not seen her there.'

He was quiet and I was quiet.

'Chicha, I think I should go away now. I have just heard that my sister has given birth to a girl.'

'So,' I smiled to myself. 'Give her my congratulations and tell her I will come to see her tomorrow.'

'*Yoo.*'

He walked away to greet his new niece. I stood for a long time at the window staring at nothing, while I heard snatches of words and phrases from the quarrel. And these were mingled with weeping. Then I turned from the window. Looking into the little mirror on the wall, I was not surprised to see my whole face bathed in unconscious tears. I did not feel like going to bed. I did not feel like doing anything at all. I toyed with the idea of going to see Maami Ama and then finally decided against it. I could not bear to face her; at least, not yet. So I sat down thinking about him. I went over the most presumptuous daydreams I had indulged in on his account. 'I would have taken him away with me in spite of his mother's protests.' She was just being absurd. 'The child is a boy, and sooner or later, she must learn to live without him. The highest class here is Primary Six and when I am going away, I will take him. I will give him a grammar education. Perhaps, who knows, one day he may win a scholarship to the university.' In my daydreams, I had never determined what career he would have followed, but he would be famous, that was certain. Devastatingly handsome, he would be the idol of women and the envy of every man. He would visit Britain, America and all those countries we have heard so much about. He would see all the seven wonders of the world. 'Maami shall be happy in the end,' I had told myself. 'People will flock to see the mother of such an illustrious man. Although she has not had many children, she will be surrounded by her grandchildren. Of course, away from the village.' In all these reveries his father never had a place, but there was I, and there was Maami Ama, and there was his father, and he, that bone of contention, was lost to all three. I saw the highest castles I had built for him come tumbling down, noiselessly and swiftly.

He was buried at four o'clock. I had taken the schoolchildren to where he lay in state. When his different relatives saw the little uniformed figure they all forgot their differences and burst into loud lamentations. 'Chicha, O Chicha, what shall I do now that Kwesi is dead?' His grandmother addressed me. 'Kwesi, my Beauty, Kwesi my Master, Kwesi-my-own-Kwesi,' one aunt was chanting, 'Father Death has done me an ill turn.'

'Chicha,' the grandmother continued, 'my washing days are over, for who will give me water? My eating days are over, for who will give me food?' I stood there, saying nothing. I had let the children sing 'Saviour Blessed Saviour'. And we had gone to the cemetery with him.

After the funeral, I went to the House of Mourning as one should do after a burial. No one was supposed to weep again for the rest of the day. I sat there listening to visitors who had come from the neighbouring villages.

'This is certainly sad, and it is most strange. School has become like business; those who found it earlier for their children are eating more than the children themselves. To have a schoolboy snatched away like this is unbearable indeed,' one woman said.

'Ah, do not speak,' his father's youngest sister broke in. 'We have lost a treasure.'

'My daughter,' said the grandmother again, 'Kwesi is gone, gone for ever to our forefathers. And what can we do?'

'What can we do indeed? When flour is scattered in the

D

sand, who can sift it? But this is the saddest I've heard, that
he was his mother's only one.'

'Is that so?' another visitor cried. 'I always thought she
had other children. What does one do, when one's only water-
pot breaks?' she whispered. The question was left hanging in
the air. No one dared say anything more.

I went out. I never knew how I got there, but I saw myself
approaching Maami Ama's hut. As usual, the door was open.
I entered the outer room. She was not there. Only sheep and
goats from the village were busy munching at the cassava and
the yams. I looked into the inner chamber. She was there. Still
clad in the cloth she had worn to the divorce proceedings, she
was not sitting, standing or lying down. She was kneeling, and
like one drowning who catches at a straw, she was clutching
Kwesi's books and school uniform to her breast. 'Maami Ama,
Maami Ama,' I called out to her. She did not move. I left
her alone. Having driven the sheep and goats away, I went
out, shutting the door behind me. 'I must go home now,' I
spoke to myself once more. The sun was sinking behind the
coconut palm. I looked at my watch. It was six o'clock; but
this time, I did not run.

A Gift from Somewhere

The Mallam had been to the village once. A long time ago. A long time ago, he had come to do these parts with Ahmadu. That had been his first time. He did not remember what had actually happened except that Ahmadu had died one night during the trip. Allah, the things that can happen to us in our exile and wanderings!

Now the village was quiet. But these people. How can they leave their villages so empty every day like this? Any time you come to a village in these parts in the afternoon, you only find the too young, the too old, the maimed and the dying, or else goats and chickens, never men and women. They don't have any cause for alarm. There is no fighting here, no marauding.

He entered several compounds which were completely deserted. Then he came to this one and saw the woman. Pointing to her stomach, he said, 'Mami Fanti, there is something there.' The woman started shivering. He was embarrassed.

Something told him that there was nothing wrong with the woman herself. Perhaps there was a baby? Oh Allah, one always has to make such violent guesses. He looked round for a stool. When he saw one lying by the wall, he ran to pick it up. He returned with it to where the woman was sitting, placed it right opposite her, and sat down.

Then he said, 'Mami, by Allah, by his holy prophet Mohamet, let your heart rest quiet in your breast. This little one, this child, he will live . . .'

And she lifted her head which until then was so bent her chin touched her breasts, and raised her eyes to the face of the Mallam for the first time, and asked 'Papa Kramo, is that true?'

'Ah Mami Fanti,' the Mallam rejoined. 'Mm . . . mm,' shaking awhile the forefinger of his right hand. This movement accompanied simultaneously as it was by his turbanned head and face, made him look very knowing indeed.

'Mm . . . mm, and why must you yourself be asking me if it is true? Have I myself lied to you before, eh Mami Fanti?'

'Hmmmm. . . .' sighed she of the anxious heart. 'It is just that I cannot find it possible to believe that he will live. That is why I asked you that.'

His eyes glittered with the pleasure of his first victory and her heart did a little somersault.

'Mami Fanti, I myself, me, I am telling you. The little one, he will live. Now today he may not look good, perhaps not today. Perhaps even after eight days he will not be good but I tell you, Mami, one moon, he will be good . . . good . . . good,' and he drew up his arms, bent them, contracted his shoulders and shook up the upper part of his body to indicate how well and strong he thought the child would be. It was a beautiful sight and for an instant a smile passed over her face. But the smile was not able to stay. It was chased away by the anxiety that seemed to have come to occupy her face forever.

'Papa Kramo, if you say that, I believe you. But you will give me something to protect him from the witches?'

'Mami Fanti, you yourself you are in too much hurry, and why? Have I got up to go?'

She shook her head and said 'No' with a voice that quaked with fear.

'Aha . . . so you yourself you must be patient. I myself will do everything . . . everything. . . . Allah is present and Mohamet his holy prophet is here too. I will do everything for you. You hear?'

She breathed deeply and loudly in reply.

'Now bring to me the child.' She stood up, and unwound the other cloth with which she had so far covered up her bruised soul and tied it around her waist. She turned in her step and knocked over the stool. The clanging noise did not attract her attention in the least. Slowly, she walked towards the door. The Mallam's eyes followed her while his left hand groped through the folds of his boubou in search of his last piece of cola. Then he remembered that his sack was still on his shoulder. He removed it, placed it on the floor and now with both his hands free, he fished out the cola. He popped it into his mouth and his tongue received the bitter piece of fruit with the eagerness of a lover.

The stillness of the afternoon was yet to be broken. In the hearth, a piece of coal yielded its tiny ash to the naughty breeze, blinked with its last spark and folded itself up in death. Above, a lonely cloud passed over the Mallam's turban, on its way to join camp in the south. And as if the Mallam had felt the motion of the cloud, he looked up and scanned the sky.

Perhaps it shall rain tonight? I must hurry up with this woman so that I can reach the next village before nightfall.

'Papa Kramo-e-e –!'

This single cry pierced through the dark interior of the room in which the child was lying, hit the aluminium utensils in the outer room, gathered itself together, cut through the silence of that noon, and echoed in the several corners of the village. The Mallam sprang up. 'What is it, Mami Fanti?' And the two collided at the door to her rooms. But neither of them saw how she managed to throw the baby on him and how he came to himself sufficiently to catch it. But the world is a wonderful place and such things happen in it daily. The Mallam caught the baby before it fell.

'Look, look, Papa Kramo, look! Look and see if this baby is not dead. See if this baby too is not dead. Just look – o – o Papa Kramo, look!' And she started running up and down, jumping, wringing her hands and undoing the threads in her

hair. Was she immediately mad? Perhaps. The only way to
tell that a possessed woman of this kind is not completely out
of her senses is that she does not uncloth herself to naked-
ness. The Mallam was bewildered.

'Mami Fanti, *hei*, Mami Fanti,' he called unheeded. Then
he looked down at the child in his arms.

Allah, tch, tch, tch. Now, O holy Allah. Now only you can
rescue me from this trouble, since my steps found this house
guided by the Prophet, but Allah, this baby is dead.

And he looked down again at it to confirm his suspicion.

Allah, the child is breathing but what kind of breath is this?
I must hurry up and leave. Ah . . . what a bad day this is.
But I will surely not want the baby to grow still in my arms!
At all . . . for that will be bad luck, big bad luck. . . . And now
where is its mother? This is not good. I am so hungry now.
I thought at least I was going to earn some four pennies so I
could eat. I do not like to go without food when it is not
Ramaddan. Now look – And I can almost count its ribs! One,
two, three, four, five. . . . And Ah . . . llah, it is pale. I could
swear this is a Fulani child only its face does not show that
it is. If this is the pallor of sickness . . . O Mohamet! Now I
must think up something quickly to comfort the mother
with.

'*Hei* Mami Fanti, Mami Fanti!'

'Papaa!'

"Come.'

She danced in from the doorway still wringing her hands
and sucking in the air through her mouth like one who had
swallowed a mouthful of scalding-hot porridge.

'It is dead, is it not?' she asked with the courtesy of the
insane.

'Mami, sit down.'

She sat.

'Mami, what is it yourself you are doing? Yourself you
make plenty noise. It is not good. Eh, what is it for yourself
you do that?'

Not knowing how to answer the questions, she kept quiet. 'Yourself, look well.' She craned her neck as though she were looking for an object in a distance. She saw his breath flutter.

'Yourself you see he is not dead?'

'Yes,' she replied without conviction. It was too faint a breath to build any hopes on, but she did not say this to the Mallam.

'Now listen Mami,' he said, and he proceeded to spit on the child: once on his forehead and then on his navel. Then he spat into his right palm and with this spittle started massaging the child very hard on his joints, the neck, shoulder blades, ankles and wrists. You could see he was straining himself very hard. You would have thought the child's skin would peel off any time. And the woman could not bear to look on.

If the child had any life in him, surely, he could have yelled at least once more? She sank her chin deeper into her breast.

'Now Mami, I myself say, you yourself, you must listen.'

'Papa, I am listening.'

'Mami, I myself say, this child will live. Now himself he is too small. Yourself you must not eat meat. You must not eat fish from the sea, Friday, Sunday. You hear?' She nodded in reply. 'He himself, if he is about ten years,' and he counted ten by flicking the five fingers of his left hand twice over, 'if he is about ten, tell him he must not eat meat and fish from the sea, Friday, Sunday. If he himself he does not eat, you Mami Fanti, you can eat. You hear?'

She nodded again.

'Now, the child he will live, yourself you must stop weeping. If you do that it is not good. Now you have the blue dye for washing?'

'Yes,' she murmured.

'And a piece of white cloth?'

'Yes, but it is not big. Just about a yard and a quarter.'

'That does not matter. Yourself, find those things for me and I will do something and your child he shall be good.'

She did not say anything.

'Did you yourself hear me, Mami Fanti?'

'Yes.'

'Now take the child, put him in the room. Come back, go and find all the things.'

She took the thing which might once have been a human child but now was certainly looking like something else and went back with it to the room.

And she was thinking.

Who does the Mallam think he is deceiving? This is the third child to die. The others never looked half this sick. No! In fact the last one was fat. . . . I had been playing with it. After the evening meal I had laid him down on the mat to go and take a quick bath. Nothing strange in that. When I returned to the house later, I powdered myself and finished up the last bits of my toilet. . . . When I eventually went in to pick up my baby, he was dead.

. . . O my Lord, my Mighty God, who does the Mallam think he is deceiving?

And he was thinking.

Ah . . . llah just look, I cannot remain here. It will be bad of me to ask the woman for so much as a penny when I know this child will die. Ah . . . llah, look, the day has come a long way and I have still not eaten.

He rose up, picked up his bag from the ground and with a quietness and swiftness of which only a nomad is capable, he vanished from the house. When the woman had laid the child down, she returned to the courtyard.

'Papa Kramo, Papa Kramo,' she called. A goat who had been lying nearby chewing the cud got up and went out quietly too.

'Kramo, Kramo,' only her own voice echoed in her brain. She sat down again on the stool. If she was surprised at all, it was only at the neatness of his escape. So he too had seen death.

Should any of my friends hear me moaning, they will say

I am behaving like one who has not lost a baby before, like a fresh bride who sees her first baby dying. Now all I must do is to try and prepare myself for another pregnancy, for it seems this is the reason why I was created . . . to be pregnant for nine of the twelve months of every year. . . . Or is there a way out of it at all? And where does this road lie? I shall have to get used to it. . . . It is the pattern set for my life. For the moment, I must be quiet until the mothers come back in the evening to bury him.

Then rewrapping the other cloth around her shoulders, she put her chin in her breast and she sat, as though the Mallam had never been there.

. . . . .

But do you know, this child did not die. It is wonderful but this child did not die. Mmm. . . . This strange world always has something to surprise us with . . . Kweku Nyamekye. Somehow, he did not die. To his day name Kweku, I have added Nyamekye. Kweku Nyamekye. For, was he not a gift from God through the Mallam of the Bound Mouth? And he, the Mallam of the Bound Mouth, had not taken from me a penny, not a single penny that ever bore a hole. And the way he had vanished! Or it was perhaps the god who yielded me to my mother who came to my aid at last? As he had promised her he would? I remember Maame telling me that when I was only a baby, the god of Mbemu from whom I came, had promised never to desert me and that he would come to me once in my life when I needed him most. And was it not him who had come in the person of the Mallam? . . . But was it not strange, the way he disappeared without asking for a penny? He had not even waited for me to buy the things he had prescribed. He was going to make a charm. It is good that he did not, for how can a scholar go through life wearing something like that? Looking at the others of the Bound Mouth, sometimes you can spot familiar faces, but my Mallam has never been here again.

Nyamekye, hmm, and after him I have not lost any more children. Let me touch wood. In this world, it is true, there is always something somewhere, covered with leaves. Nyamekye lived. I thought his breathing would have stopped, by the time the old women returned in the evening. But it did not. Towards nightfall his colour changed completely.He did not feel so hot. His breathing improved and from then, he grew stronger every day. But if ever I come upon the Mallam, I will just fall down before him, wipe his tired feet with a silk kente, and then spread it before him and ask him to walk on it. If I do not do that then no one should call me Abena Gyaawa again.

When he started recovering, I took up the taboo as the Mallam had instructed. He is now going to be eleven years old I think. Eleven years, and I have never, since I took it up, missed observing it any Friday or Sunday. Not once. Sometimes I wonder why he chose these two days and not others. If my eyes had not been scattered about me that afternoon, I would have asked him to explain the reason behind this choice to me. And now I shall never know.

Yes, eleven years. But it has been difficult. Oh, it is true I do not think that I am one of these women with a sweet tooth for fish and meats. But if you say that you are going to eat soup, then it is soup you are going to eat. Perhaps no meat or fish may actually hit your teeth but how can you say any broth has soul when it does not contain anything at all? It is true that like everyone else, I liked kontomire. But like everyone else too, I ate it only when my throat ached for it or when I was on the farm. But since I took up the taboo, I have had to eat it at least twice two days of the week, Sunday and Friday. I have come to hate its deep-green look. My only relief came with the season of snails and mushrooms. But everyone knows that these days they are getting rarer because it does not rain as often as it used to. Then after about five years of this strict observance, someone who knew about these things advised me. He said that since the Mallam had mentioned the sea, at least I could eat freshwater fish or prawns and crabs. I did not like the idea of eating fish at all. Who can tell which minnow has paid a visit to the ocean? So I began eating fresh-water prawns and crabs – but of course, only when I could get them. Normally, you do not get these things unless you have a grown-up son who would go trapping in the river for you.

But I do not mind these difficulties. If the Mallam came back to tell me that I must stop eating fish and meat alto-gether so that Nyamekye and the others would live, I would do it. I would. After all, he had told me that I could explain the taboo to Nyamekye when he was old enough to under-stand, so he could take it up himself. But I have not done it and I do not think I shall ever do it. How can a schoolboy, and who knows, one day he may become a real scholar, how can he go through life dragging this type of taboo along with him? I have never heard any scholar doing it, and my son is not going to be first to do it. No. I myself will go on observing it until I die. For, how could I have gone on living with my two empty hands? – I swear by everything, I do not understand people who complain that I am spoiling them, especially him. And anyway, is it any business of theirs? Even if I daily anointed them with shea-butter and placed them in the sun, whom would I hurt? Who else should be concerned apart from me?

But the person whose misunderstanding hurts me is their father. I do not know what to do. Something tells me it's his people and his wives who prevent him from having good thoughts about me and mine. I was his first wife and if you knew how at the outset of our lives, death haunted us, hmmm. Neither of us had a head to think in. And if things were what they should be, should he be behaving in this way? In fact, I swear by everything, he hates Nyamekye. Or how could what happened last week have happened?

It was a Friday and they had not gone to school. It was a holiday for them. I do not know what this one was for but it was one of those days they do not go. When the time came for us to leave for the farm, I showed him where food was and asked him to look after himself and his younger brother and sisters. Well my tongue was still moving when his father came in with his face shut down, the way it is when he is angry. He came up to us and asked '*Hei*, Nyamekye, are you not following your mother to the farm?' Oh, I was hurt. Is this the way to talk to a ten-year-old child? If he had been any other father, he would have said, 'Nyamekye, since you are not going to school today, pick up your knife and come with me to the farm.'

Would that not have been beautiful?

'Nyamekye, are you not following your mother to the farm?' As if I am the boy's only parent. But he is stuck with this habit, especially where I and my little ones are concerned.

'Gyaawa, your child is crying. . . . Gyaawa, your child is going to fall off the terrace if you do not pay more attention to him. . . . Gyaawa, your child this, and your child that!'

Anyway, that morning I was hurt and when I opened up my mouth, all the words which came to my lips were, 'I thought this boy was going to be a scholar and not a farm-goer. What was the use in sending him to school if I knew he was going to follow me to the farm?'

This had made him more angry. 'I did not know that if you go to school, your skin must not touch a leaf!'

I did not say anything. What had I to say? We went to the farm leaving Nyamekye with the children. I returned home earlier than his father did. Nyamekye was not in the house. I asked his brother and sisters if they knew where he had gone. But they had not seen him since they finished eating earlier in the afternoon. When he had not come home by five o'clock, I started getting worried. Then his father too returned from the farm. He learned immediately that he was missing. He clouded up. After he had had his bath, he went to sit in his chair, dark as a rainy sky. Then he got up to go by the chicken coop. I did not know that he was going to fetch a cane. Just as he was sitting in the chair again, Nyamekye appeared.

'*Hei*, Kweku Nyamekye, come here.'

Nyamekye was holding the little bucket and I knew where he had been to. He moved slowly up to his father.

'Papa, I went to the river to visit my trap, because today is Friday.'

'Have I asked you for anything? And your traps! Is that what you go to school to learn?'

And then he pulled out the cane and fell on the child. The bucket dropped and a few little prawns fell out. Something tells me it was the sight of those prawns which finished his father. He poured those blows on him as though he were made of wood. I had made up my mind never to interfere in any manner he chose to punish the children, for after all, they are his too. But this time I thought he was going too far. I rushed out to rescue Nyamekye and then it came, wham! The sharpest blow I have ever received in my life caught me on the inside of my arm. Blood gushed out. When he saw what had happened, he was ashamed. He went away into his room. That evening he did not eat the fufu I served him.

Slowly, I picked up the bucket and the prawns. Nyamekye followed me to my room where I wept.

The scar healed quickly but the scar is of the type which rises so anyone can see it. Nyamekye's father's attitude has changed towards us. He is worse. He is angry all the time. He is angry with shame.

But I do not even care. I have my little ones. And I am sure someone is wishing she were me. I have Nyamekye. And for this, I do not even know whom to thank.

'Do I thank you, O Mallam of the Bound Mouth?

Or you, Nana Mbemu, since I think you came in the person of the Mallam?

Or Mighty Jehovah-after-whom-there-is-none-other, to you alone should I give my thanks?

But why should I let this worry me? I thank you all. Oh, I thank you all. And you, our ancestral spirits, if you are looking after me, then look after the Mallam too. Remember him at meals, for he is a kinsman.

And as for this scar, I am glad it is not on Nyamekye. Any time I see it I only recall one afternoon when I sat with my chin in my breast before a Mallam came in, and after a Mallam went out.

Two Sisters

As she shakes out the typewriter cloak and covers the machine with it, the thought of the bus she has to hurry to catch goes through her like a pain. It is her luck, she thinks. Everything is just her luck. Why, if she had one of those graduates for a boy-friend, wouldn't he come and take her home every evening? And she knows that a girl does not herself have to be a graduate to get one of those boys. Certainly, Joe is dying to do exactly that – with his taxi. And he is as handsome as anything, and a good man, but you know . . . Besides there are cars and there are cars. As for the possibility of the other actually coming to fetch her – oh well. She has to admit it will take some time before she can bring herself to make demands of that sort on *him*. She has also to admit that the temptation is extremely strong. Would it really be so dangerously indiscreet? Doesn't one government car look like another? The hugeness of it? Its shaded glass? The uniformed chauffeur? She can already see herself stepping out to greet the dead-with-envy glances of the other girls. To begin with, she will insist on a little discretion. The driver can drop her under the neem trees in the morning and pick her up from there in the evening . . . anyway, she will have to wait a little while for that and it is all her luck.

There are other ways, surely. One of these, for some reason, she has sworn to have nothing of. Her boss has a car and does not look bad. In fact the man is alright. But she keeps telling herself that she does not fancy having some old and dried-out housewife walking into the office one afternoon to tear her hair out and make a row. . . . Mm, so for the meantime, it is going to continue to be the municipal bus with its grimy seats, its common passengers and impudent conductors. . . . Jesus! She doesn't wish herself dead or anything as stupidly final as that. Oh no. She just wishes she could sleep deep and only wake up on the morning of her glory.

The new pair of black shoes are more realistic than their owner, though. As she walks down the corridor, they sing:

> *Count, Mercy, count your blessings*
> *Count, Mercy, count your blessings*
> *Count, count, count your blessings.*

They sing along the corridor, into the avenue, across the road and into the bus. And they resume their song along the gravel path, as she opens the front gate and crosses the cemented courtyard to the door.

'Sissie!' she called.

'*Hei* Mercy,' and the door opened to show the face of Connie, big sister, six years or more older and now heavy with her second child. Mercy collapsed into the nearest chair.

'Welcome home. How was the office today?'

'Sister, don't ask. Look at my hands. My fingers are dead with typing. Oh God, I don't know what to do.'

'Why, what is wrong?'

'You tell me what is right. Why should I be a typist?'

'What else would you be?'

'What a strange question. Is typing the only thing one can do in this world? You are a teacher, are you not?'

'But . . . but . . .'

'But what? Or you want me to know that if I had done better in the exams, I could have trained to be a teacher too, eh, sister? Or even a proper secretary?'

'Mercy, what is the matter? What have I done? What have I done? Why have you come home so angry?'

Mercy broke into tears.

'Oh I am sorry. I am sorry, Sissie. It's just that I am sick of everything. The office, living with you and your husband. I want a husband of my own, children. I want . . . I want . . .'

'But you are so beautiful.'

'Thank you. But so are you.'

'You are young and beautiful. As for marriage, it's you who are postponing it. Look at all these people who are running after you.'

'Sissie, I don't like what you are doing. So stop it.'

'Okay, okay, okay.'

And there was a silence.

'Which of them could I marry? Joe is – mm, fine – but, but I just don't like him.'

'You mean . . .'

'Oh, Sissie!'

'Little sister, you and I can be truthful with one another.'

'Oh yes.'

'What I would like to say is that I am not that old or wise. But still I could advise you a little. Joe drives someone's car now. Well, you never know. Lots of taxi drivers come to own their taxis, sometimes fleets of cars.'

'Of course. But it's a pity you are married already. Or I could be a go-between for you and Joe!'

And the two of them burst out laughing. It was when she rose to go to the bedroom that Connie noticed the new shoes.

'*Ei*, those are beautiful shoes. Are they new?'

From the other room, Mercy's voice came interrupted by the motions of her body as she undressed and then dressed again. However, the uncertainty in it was due to something entirely different.

'Oh, I forgot to tell you about them. In fact, I was going to show them to you. I think it was on Tuesday I bought them. Or was it Wednesday? When I came home from the office, you and James had taken Akosua out. And later, I forgot all about them.'

'I see. But they are very pretty. Were they expensive?'

'No, not really.' This reply was too hurriedly said.

And she said only last week that she didn't have a penny on her. And I believed her because I know what they pay her is just not enough to last anyone through any month, even minus rent. . . . I have been thinking she manages very well. But these shoes. And she is not the type who would borrow money just to buy a pair of shoes, when she could have gone on wearing her old pairs until things get better. Oh I wish I knew what to do. I mean I am not her mother. And I wonder how James will see these problems.

'Sissie, you look worried.'

'Hmm, when don't I? With the baby due in a couple of months and the government's new ruling on salaries and all. On top of everything, I have reliable information that James is running after a new girl.'

Mercy laughed.

'Oh Sissie. You always get reliable information on these things.'

'But yes. And I don't know why.'

'Sissie, men are like that.'

'They are selfish.'

'No, it's just that women allow them to behave the way they do instead of seizing some freedom themselves.'

'But I am sure that even if we were free to carry on in the same way, I wouldn't make use of it.'

'But why not?'

'Because I love James. I love James and I am not interested in any other man.' Her voice was full of tears. But Mercy was amused.

'O God. Now listen to that. It's women like you who keep all of us down.'

'Well, I am sorry but it's how the good God created me.'

'Mm. I am sure that I can love several men at the same time.'

'Mercy!'

They burst out laughing again. And yet they are sad. But laughter is always best.

Mercy complained of hunger and so they went to the kitchen to heat up some food and eat. The two sisters alone. It is no use waiting for James. And this evening, a friend of Connie's has come to take out the baby girl, Akosua, and had threatened to keep her until her bedtime.

'Sissie, I am going to see a film.' This from Mercy.

'Where?'

'The Globe.'

'Are you going with Joe?'

'No.'

'Are you going alone?'

'No.'

Careful Connie.

'Whom are you going with?'

Careful Connie, please. Little sister's nostrils are widening dangerously. Look at the sudden creasing-up of her mouth and between her brows. Connie, a sister is a good thing. Even a younger sister. Especially when you have no mother or father.

'Mercy, whom are you going out with?'

'Well, I had food in my mouth! And I had to swallow it down before I could answer you, no?'

'I am sorry.' How softly said.

'And anyway, do I have to tell you everything?'

'Oh no. It's just that I didn't think it was a question I should not have asked.'

There was more silence. Then Mercy sucked her teeth with irritation and Connie cleared her throat with fear.

'I am going out with Mensar-Arthur.'

As Connie asked the next question, she wondered if the words were leaving her lips.

'Mensar-Arthur?'

'Yes.'
'Which one?'
'How many do you know?'
Her fingers were too numb to pick up the food. She put the plate down. Something jumped in her chest and she wondered what it was. Perhaps it was the baby.
'Do you mean that member of Parliament?'
'Yes.'
'But Mercy . . .'
Little sister only sits and chews her food.
'But Mercy . . .'
Chew, chew, chew.
'But Mercy . . .'
'What?'
She startled Connie.
'He is so old.'
Chew, chew, chew.
'Perhaps, I mean, perhaps that really doesn't matter, does it? Not very much anyway. But they say he has so many wives and girl-friends.'
Please little sister. I am not trying to interfere in your private life. You said yourself a little while ago that you wanted a man of your own. That man belongs to so many women already. . . .
That silence again. Then there was only Mercy's footsteps as she went to put her plate in the kitchen sink, running water as she washed her plate and her hands. She drank some water and coughed. Then as tears streamed down her sister's averted face, there was the sound of her footsteps as she left the kitchen. At the end of it all, she banged a door. Connie only said something like, 'O Lord, O Lord,' and continued sitting in the kitchen. She had hardly eaten anything at all. Very soon Mercy went to have a bath. Then Connie heard her getting ready to leave the house. The shoes. Then she was gone. She needn't have carried on like that, eh? Because Connie had not meant to probe or bring on a quarrel. What use is there in this

old world for a sister, if you can't have a chat with her? What's more, things like this never happen to people like Mercy. Their parents were good Presbyterians. They feared God. Mama had not managed to give them all the rules of life before she died. (But Connie knows that running around with an old and depraved public man would have been considered an abomination by the parents.)

A big car with a super-smooth engine purred into the drive. It actually purrs: this huge machine from the white man's land. Indeed, its well-mannered protest as the tyres slid on to the gravel seemed like a lullaby compared to the loud thumping of the girl's stiletto shoes. When Mensar-Arthur saw Mercy, he stretched his arm and opened the door to the passenger seat. She sat down and the door closed with a civilised thud. The engine hummed into motion and the car sailed away.

After a distance of a mile or so from the house, the man started conversation.

'And how is my darling today?'

'I am well,' and only the words did not imply tragedy.

'You look solemn today, why?'

She remained silent and still.

'My dear, what is the matter?'

'Nothing.'

'Oh . . .' he cleared his throat again. 'Eh, and how were the shoes?'

'Very nice. In fact, I am wearing them now. They pinch a little but then all new shoes are like that.'

'And the handbag?'

'I like it very much too. . . . My sister noticed them. I mean the shoes.' The tragedy was announced.

'Did she ask you where you got them from?'

'No.'

He cleared his throat again.

'Where did we agree to go tonight?'

'The Globe, but I don't want to see a film.'

'Is that so? Mm, I am glad because people always notice things.'

'But they won't be too surprised.'

'What are you saying, my dear?'

'Nothing.'

'Okay, so what shall we do?'

'I don't know.'

'Shall I drive to the Seaway?'

'Oh yes.'

He drove to the Seaway. To a section of the beach they knew very well. She loves it here. This wide expanse of sand and the old sea. She has often wished she could do what she fancied: one thing she fancies. Which is to drive very near to the end of the sands until the tyres of the car touched the water. Of course it is a very foolish idea as he pointed out sharply to her the first time she thought aloud about it. It was in his occasional I-am-more-than-old-enough-to-be-your-father tone. There are always disadvantages. Things could be different. Like if one had a younger lover. Handsome, maybe not rich like this man here, but well-off, sufficiently well-off to be able to afford a sports car. A little something very much like those in the films driven by the white racing drivers. With tyres that can do everything . . . and they would drive exactly where the sea and the sand meet.

'We are here.'

'Don't let's get out. Let's just sit inside and talk.'

'Talk?'

'Yes.'

'Okay. But what is it, my darling?'

'I have told my sister about you.'

'Good God. Why?'

'But I had to. I couldn't keep it to myself any longer.'

'Childish. It was not necessary at all. She is not your mother.'

'No. But she is all I have. And she has been very good to me.'

'Well, it was her duty.'

'Then it is my duty to tell her about something like this. I may get into trouble.'

'Don't be silly,' he said, 'I normally take good care of my girl-friends.'

'I see,' she said and for the first time in the one month since she agreed to be this man's lover, the tears which suddenly rose into her eyes were not forced.

'And you promised you wouldn't tell her.' It was father's voice now.

'Don't be angry. After all, people talk so much, as you said a little while ago. She was bound to hear it one day.'

'My darling, you are too wise. What did she say?'

'She was pained.'

'Don't worry. Find out something she wants very much but cannot get in this country because of the import restrictions.'

'I know for sure she wants an electric motor for her sewing machine.'

'Is that all?'

'That's what I know of.'

'Mm. I am going to London next week on some delegation, so if you bring me the details on the make of the machine, I shall get her the motor.'

'Thank you.'

'What else is worrying my Black Beauty?'

'Nothing.'

'And by the way, let me know as soon as you want to leave your sister's place. I have got you one of the government estate houses.'

'Oh . . . oh,' she said, pleased, contented for the first time since this typically ghastly day had begun, at half-past six in the morning.

Dear little child came back from the playground with her toe bruised. Shall we just blow cold air from our mouth on it or put on a salve? Nothing matters really. Just see that she does not feel unattended. And the old sea roars on. This is a calm sea, generally. Too calm in fact, this Gulf of Guinea. The

natives sacrifice to him on Tuesdays and once a year celebrate
him. They might save their chickens, their eggs and their
yams. And as for the feast once a year, he doesn't pay much
attention to it either. They are always celebrating one thing
or another and they surely don't need him for an excuse to
celebrate one day more. He has seen things happen along these
beaches. Different things. Contradictory things. Or just repe-
titions of old patterns. He never interferes in their affairs.
Why should he? Except in places like Keta where he eats
houses away because they leave him no choice. Otherwise he
never allows them to see his passions. People are worms, and
even the God who created them is immensely bored with their
antics. Here is a fifty-year-old 'big man' who thinks he is
somebody. And a twenty-three-year-old child who chooses
a silly way to conquer unconquerable problems. Well, what
did one expect of human beings? And so as those two settled
on the back seat of the car to play with each other's bodies, he,
the Gulf of Guinea, shut his eyes with boredom. It is right.
He could sleep, no? He spread himself and moved further
ashore. But the car was parked at a very safe distance and the
rising tides could not wet its tyres.

James has come home late. But then he has been coming back
late for the past few weeks. Connie is crying and he knows it
as soon as he enters the bedroom. He hates tears, for like so
many men, he knows it is one of the most potent weapons in
women's bitchy and inexhaustible arsenal. She speaks first.

'James.'

'Oh, you are still awake?' He always tries to deal with these
nightly funeral parlour doings by pretending not to know what
they are about.

'I couldn't sleep.'

'What is wrong?'

'Nothing.'

So he moves quickly and sits beside her.

'Connie, what is the matter? You have been crying again.'

'You are very late again.'

'Is that why you are crying? Or is there something else?'

'Yes.'

'Yes to what?'

'James, where were you?'

'Connie, I have warned you about what I shall do if you don't stop examining me, as though I were your prisoner, every time I am a little late.'

She sat up.

'A little late! It is nearly two o'clock.'

'Anyway, you won't believe me if I told you the truth, so why do you want me to waste my breath?'

'Oh well.' She lies down again and turns her face to the wall. He stands up but does not walk away. He looks down at her. So she remembers every night: they have agreed, after many arguments, that she should sleep like this. During her first pregnancy, he kept saying after the third month or so that the sight of her tummy the last thing before he slept always gave him nightmares. Now he regrets all this. The bed creaks as he throws himself down by her.

'James.'

'Yes.'

'There is something much more serious.'

'You have heard about my newest affair?'

'Yes, but that is not what I am referring to.'

'Jesus, is it possible that there is anything more important than that?'

And as they laugh they know that something has happened. One of those things which, with luck, will keep them together for some time to come.

'He teases me on top of everything.'

'What else can one do to you but tease when you are in this state?'

'James! How profane!'

'It is your dirty mind which gave my statement its shocking meaning.'

'Okay! But what shall I do?'

'About what?'

'Mercy. Listen, she is having an affair with Mensar-Arthur.'

'Wonderful.'

She sits up and he sits up.

'James, we must do something about it. It is very serious.'

'Is that why you were crying?'

'Of course.'

'Why shouldn't she?'

'But it is wrong. And she is ruining herself.'

'Since every other girl she knows has ruined herself prosperously, why shouldn't she? Just forget for once that you are a teacher. Or at least, remember she is not your pupil.'

'I don't like your answers.'

'What would you like me to say? Every morning her friends who don't earn any more than she does wear new dresses, shoes, wigs and what-have-you to work. What would you have her do?'

'The fact that other girls do it does not mean that Mercy should do it too.'

'You are being very silly. If I were Mercy, I am sure that's exactly what I would do. And you know I mean it too.'

James is cruel. He is terrible and mean. Connie breaks into fresh tears and James comforts her. There is one point he must drive home though.

'In fact, encourage her. He may be able to intercede with the Ministry for you so that after the baby is born they will not transfer you from here for some time.'

'James, you want me to use my sister!'

'She is using herself, remember.'

'James, you are wicked.'

'And maybe he would even agree to get us a new car from abroad. I shall pay for everything. That would be better than paying a fortune for that old thing I was thinking of buying. Think of that.'

'You will ride in it alone.'

'Well . . .'

That was a few months before the *coup*. Mensar-Arthur
did go to London for a conference and bought something for
all his wives and girl-friends, including Mercy. (He even
remembered the motor for Connie's machine. When Mercy
took it to her she was quite confused. She had wanted this
thing for a long time, and it would make everything so much
easier, like the clothes for the new baby. And yet one side of
her said that accepting it was a betrayal.)Of what, she wasn't
even sure. She and Mercy could never bring the whole business into the open and discuss it. And there was always James
supporting Mercy, to Connie's bewilderment. She took the
motor with thanks and sold even her right to dissent. In a
short while, Mercy left the house to go and live in the estate
house Mensar-Arthur had procured for her. Then, a couple
of weeks later, the *coup*. Mercy left her new place before
anyone could evict her. James never got his car. Connie's
new baby was born. Of the three, the one who greeted the new
order with undisguised relief was Connie. She is not really a
demonstrative person but it was obvious from her eyes that
she was happy. As far as she was concerned, the old order as
symbolised by Mensar-Arthur was a threat to her sister and
therefore to her own peace of mind. With it gone, things could
return to normal. Mercy would move back to the house,
perhaps start to date someone more – ordinary, let's say.
Eventually, she would get married and then the nightmare of
those past weeks would be forgotten. God being so good, he
brought the *coup* early before the news of the affair could
spread and brand her sister. . . .

The arrival of the new baby has magically waved away the
difficulties between James and Connie. He is that kind of man,
and she that kind of woman. Mercy has not been seen for
many days. Connie is beginning to get worried. . . .

James heard the baby yelling – a familiar noise, by now – the
moment he opened the front gate. He ran in, clutching to his
chest the few things he had bought on his way home.

'We are in here.'

'I certainly could hear you. If there is anything people of this country have, it is a big mouth.'

'Don't I agree? But on the whole, we are well. He is eating normally and everything. You?'

'Nothing new. Same routine. More stories about the overthrown politicians.'

'What do you mean, nothing new? Look at the excellent job the soldiers have done, cleaning up the country of all that dirt. I feel free already and I am dying to get out and enjoy it.'

James laughed mirthlessly.

'All I know is that Mensar-Arthur is in jail. No use. And I am not getting my car. Rough deal.'

'I never took you seriously on that car business.'

'Honestly, if this were in the ancient days, I could brand you a witch. You don't want me, your husband, to prosper?'

'Not out of my sister's ruin.'

'Ruin, ruin, ruin! Christ! See Connie, the funny thing is that I am sure you are the only person who thought it was a disaster to have a sister who was the girl-friend of a big man.'

'Okay; now all is over, and don't let's quarrel.'

'I bet the *coup* could have succeeded on your prayers alone.'

And Connie wondered why he said that with so much bitterness. She wondered if . . .

'Has Mercy been here?'

'Not yet, later, maybe. Mm. I had hoped she would move back here and start all over again.'

'I am not surprised she hasn't. In fact, if I were her, I wouldn't come back here either. Not to your nagging, no thank you, big sister.'

And as the argument progressed, as always, each was forced into a more aggressive defensive stand.

'Well, just say what pleases you, I am very glad about the soldiers. Mercy is my only sister, brother; everything. I can't sit and see her life going wrong without feeling it. I am grateful to whatever forces there are which put a stop to that.

What pains me now is that she should be so vague about where she is living at the moment. She makes mention of a girl-friend but I am not sure that I know her.'

'If I were you, I would stop worrying because it seems Mercy can look after herself quite well.'

'Hmm,' was all she tried to say.

Who heard something like the sound of a car pulling into the drive? Ah, but the footsteps are unmistakably Mercy's. Are those shoes the old pair which were new a couple of months ago? Or are they the newest pair? And here she is herself, the pretty one. A gay Mercy.

'Hello, hello, my clan!' and she makes a lot of her nephew.

'Dow-dah-dee-day! And how is my dear young man to-day? My lord, grow up fast and come to take care of Auntie Mercy.'

Both Connie and James cannot take their eyes off her. Connie says, 'He says to Auntie Mercy he is fine.'

Still they watch her, horrified, fascinated and wondering what it's all about. Because they both know it is about something.'

'Listen people, I brought a friend to meet you. A man.'

'Where is he?' from James.

'Bring him in,' from Connie.

'You know, Sissie, you are a new mother. I thought I'd come and ask you if it's all right.'

'Of course,' say James and Connie, and for some reason they are both very nervous.

'He is Captain Ashey.'

'Which one?'

'*How many do you know?*'

James still thinks it is impossible. 'Eh . . . do you mean the officer who has been appointed the . . . the . . .'

'Yes.'

'Wasn't there a picture in *The Crystal* over the week-end about his daughter's wedding? And another one of him with his wife and children and grandchildren?'

'Yes.'

'And he is heading a commission to investigate something or other?'

'Yes.'

Connie just sits there with her mouth open that wide. . . .

The Late Bud

'The good child who willingly goes on errands eats the food of peace.' This was a favourite saying in the house. Maami, Aunt Efua, Aunt Araba . . . oh, they all said it, especially when they had prepared something delicious like cocoyam porridge and seasoned beef. You know how it is.

First, as they stirred it with the ladle, its scent rose from the pot and became a little cloud hanging over the hearth. Gradually, it spread through the courtyard and entered the inner and outer rooms of the women's apartments. This was the first scent that greeted the afternoon sleeper. She stretched herself luxuriously, inhaled a large quantity of the sweet scent, cried 'Mm' and either fell back again to sleep or got up to be about her business. The aroma did not stay. It rolled into the next house and the next, until it filled the whole neighbourhood. And Yaaba would sniff it.

As usual, she would be playing with her friends by the Big Trunk. She would suddenly throw down her pebbles even if it was her turn, jump up, shake her cloth free of sand and announce, 'I am going home.'

'Why?'

'Yaaba, why?'

But the questions of her amazed companions would reach her faintly like whispers. She was flying home. Having crossed the threshold, she then slunk by the wall. But there would be none for her.

Yaaba never stayed at home to go on an errand. Even when she was around, she never would fetch water to save a dying soul. How could she then eat the food of peace? Oh, if it was a formal meal, like in the morning or evening, that was a different matter. Of that, even Yaaba got her lawful share. . . . But not this sweet-sweet porridge. 'Nsia, Antobam, Naa-banyin, Adwoa, come for some porridge.' And the other children trooped in with their little plates and bowls. But not the figure by the wall. They chattered as they came and the mother teased as she dished out their titbits.

'Is yours alright, Adwoa? . . . and yours, Tawia? . . . yours is certainly sufficient, Antobam. . . . But my child, this is only a titbit for us, the deserving. Other people,' and she would squint at Yaaba, 'who have not worked will not get the tiniest bit.' She then started eating hers. If Yaaba felt that the joke was being carried too far, she coughed. 'Oh,' the mother would cry out, 'people should be careful about their throats. Even if they coughed until they spat blood none of this porridge would touch their mouths.'

But it was not things and incidents like these which worried Yaaba. For inevitably, a mother's womb cried out for a lonely figure by a wall and she would be given some porridge. Even when her mother could be bile-bellied enough to look at her and dish out all the porridge, Yaaba could run into the door-way and ambush some child and rob him of the greater part of his share. No, it was not such things that worried her. Every mother might call her a bad girl. She enjoyed playing by the Big Trunk, for instance. Since to be a good girl, one had to stay by the hearth and not by the Big Trunk throwing pebbles, but with one's hands folded quietly on one's lap, waiting to be sent everywhere by all the mothers, Yaaba let people like Adwoa who wanted to be called 'good' be good. Thank you, she was not interested.

But there was something which disturbed Yaaba. No one knew it did, but it did. She used to wonder why, every time Maami called Adwoa, she called her 'My child Adwoa', while she was always merely called 'Yaaba'.

'My child Adwoa, pick me the drinking can. . . . My child you have done well. . . .'

Oh, it is so always. Am I not my mother's child?

'Yaaba, come for your food.' She always wished in her heart that she could ask somebody about it. . . . Paapa . . . Maami . . . Nana, am I not Maami's daughter? Who was my mother?

But you see, one does not go round asking elders such questions. Take the day Antobam asked her grandmother where her own mother was. The grandmother also asked Antobam whether she was not being looked after well, and then started weeping and saying things. Other mothers joined in the weeping. Then some more women came over from the neighbourhood and her aunts and uncles came too and there was more weeping and there was also drinking and libation-pouring. At the end of it all, they gave Antobam a stiff talking-to.

No, one does not go round asking one's elders such questions.

But Adwoa, my child, bring me the knife. . . . Yaaba . . . Yaaba, your cloth is dirty. Yaaba, Yaaba . . .

It was the afternoon of the Saturday before Christmas Sunday. Yaaba had just come from the playgrounds to gobble down her afternoon meal. It was kenkey and a little fish stewed in palm oil. She had eaten in such a hurry that a bone had got stuck in her throat. She had drunk a lot of water but still the bone was sticking there. She did not want to tell Maami about it. She knew she would get a scolding or even a knock on the head. It was while she was in the outer room looking for a bit of kenkey to push down the troublesome bone that she heard Maami talking in the inner room.

'Ah, and what shall I do now? But I thought there was a whole big lump left. . . . O . . . O! Things like this irritate me so. How can I spend Christmas without varnishing my floor?'

Yaaba discovered a piece of kenkey which was left from the week before, hidden in its huge wrappings. She pounced upon it and without breaking away the mildew, swallowed it.

E

She choked, stretched her neck and the bone was gone. She drank some water and with her cloth, wiped away the tears which had started gathering in her eyes. She was about to bounce away to the playgrounds when she remembered that she had heard Maami speaking to herself.

Although one must not stand by to listen to elders if they are not addressing one, yet one can hide and listen. And anyway, it would be interesting to hear the sort of things our elders say to themselves. 'And how can I celebrate Christmas on a hardened, whitened floor?' Maami's voice went on. 'If I could only get a piece of red earth. But I cannot go round my friends begging, "Give me a piece of red earth." No. O ... O! And it is growing dark already. If only my child Adwoa was here. I am sure she could have run to the red-earth pit and fetched me just a hoeful. Then I could varnish the floor before the church bells ring tomorrow.' Yaaba was thinking she had heard enough.

After all, our elders do not say anything interesting to themselves. It is their usual complaints about how difficult life is. If it is not the price of cloth or fish, then it is the scarcity of water. It is all very uninteresting. I will always play with my children when they grow up. I will not grumble about anything. . . .

It was quite dark. The children could hardly see their own hands as they threw up the pebbles. But Yaaba insisted that they go on. There were only three left of the eight girls who were playing *soso-mba*. From time to time mothers, fathers or elder sisters had come and called to the others to go home. The two still with Yaaba were Panyin and Kakra. Their mother had travelled and that was why they were still there. No one came any longer to call Yaaba. Up till the year before, Maami always came to yell for her when it was sundown. When she could not come, she sent Adwoa. But of course, Yaaba never listened to them.

What is the point in breaking a game to go home? She stayed out and played even by herself until it was dark and she was satisfied. And now, at the age of ten, no one came to call her.

The pebble hit Kakra on the head.

'*Ajii.*'

'What is it?'

'The pebble has hit me.'

'I am sorry. It was not intentional.' Panyin said, 'But it is dark Kakra, let us go home.' So they stood up.

'Panyin, will you go to church tomorrow?'

'No.'

'Why? You have no new cloths?'

'We have new cloths but we will not get gold chains or earrings. Our mother is not at home. She has gone to some place and will only return in the afternoon. Kakra, remember we will get up very early tomorrow morning.'

'Why?'

'Have you forgotten what mother told us before she went away? Did she not tell us to go and get some red earth from the pit? Yaaba, we are going away.'

'*Yoo.*'

And the twins turned towards home.

Red earth! The pit! Probably, Maami will be the only woman in the village who will not have red earth to varnish her floor. *Oo!*

'Panyin! Kakra! Panyin!'

'Who is calling us?'

'It is me, Yaaba. Wait for me.'

She ran in the darkness and almost collided with someone who was carrying food to her husband's house.

'Panyin, do you say you will go to the pit tomorrow morning?'

'Yes, what is it?'

'I want to go with you.'

'Why?'

'Because I want to get some red earth for my mother.'

'But tomorrow you will go to church.'

'Yes, but I will try to get it done in time to go to church as well.'

'See, you cannot. Do you not know the pit? It is very far away. Everyone will already be at church by the time we get back home.'

Yaaba stood quietly digging her right toe into the hard ground beneath her. 'It doesn't matter, I will go.'

'Do you not want to wear your gold things? Kakra and I are very sorry that we cannot wear ours because our mother is not here.'

'It does not matter. Come and wake me up.'

'Where do you sleep?'

'Under my mother's window. I will wake up if you hit the window with a small pebble.'

'*Yoo*. . . . We will come to call you.'

'Do not forget your *apampa* and your hoe.'

'*Yoo*.'

When Yaaba arrived home, they had already finished eating the evening meal. Adwoa had arrived from an errand it seemed. In fact she had gone on several others. Yaaba was slinking like a cat to take her food which she knew would be under the wooden bowl, when Maami saw her. 'Yes, go and take it. You are hungry, are you not? And very soon you will be swallowing all that huge lump of fufu as quickly as a hen would swallow corn.' Yaaba stood still.

'*Aa*. My Father God, who inflicted on me such a child? Look here, Yaaba. You are growing, so be careful how you live your life. When you are ten years old you are not a child any more. And a woman that lives on the playground is not a woman. If you were a boy, it would be bad enough, but for a girl, it is a curse. The house cannot hold you. *Tchia*.'

Yaaba crept into the outer room. She saw the wooden bowl. She turned it over and as she had known all the time, her food was there. She swallowed it more quickly than a hen would have swallowed corn. When she finished eating, she went into the inner room, she picked her mat, spread it on the floor, threw herself down and was soon asleep. Long afterwards, Maami came in from the conversation with the other mothers.

When she saw the figure of Yaaba, her heart did a somersault. Pooh, went her fists on the figure in the corner. Pooh, 'You lazy lazy thing.' Pooh, pooh! 'You good-for-nothing, empty-corn husk of a daughter . . .' She pulled her ears, and Yaaba screamed. Still sleepy-eyed, she sat up on the mat.

'If you like, you scream, and watch what I will do to you. If I do not pull your mouth until it is as long as a pestle, then my name is not Benyiwa.'

But Yaaba was now wide awake and tearless. Who said she was screaming, anyway? She stared at Maami with shining tearless eyes. Maami was angry at this too.

'I spit in your eyes, witch! Stare at me and tell me if I am going to die tomorrow. At your age . . .' and the blows came pooh, pooh, pooh. 'You do not know that you wash yourself before your skin touches the mat. And after a long day in the sand, the dust and filth by the Big Trunk. *Hoo! Pooh!* You moth-bitten grain. *Pooh!*'

The clock in the chief's house struck twelve o'clock midnight. Yaaba never cried. She only tried, without success, to ward off the blows. Perhaps Maami was tired herself, perhaps she was satisfied. Or perhaps she was afraid she was putting herself in the position of Kweku Ananse tempting the spirits to carry their kindness as far as to come and help her beat her daughter. Of course, this would kill Yaaba. Anyway, she stopped beating her and lay down by Kofi, Kwame and Adwoa. Yaaba saw the figure of Adwoa lying peacefully there. It was then her eyes misted. The tears flowed from her eyes. Every time, she wiped them with her cloth but more came. They did not make any noise for Maami to hear. Soon the cloth was wet. When the clock struck one, she heard Maami snoring. She herself could not sleep even when she lay down.

Is this woman my mother?

Perhaps I should not go and fetch her some red earth. But the twins will come. . . .

Yaaba rose and went into the outer room. There was no door between the inner and outer rooms to creak and wake

109

anybody. She wanted the *apampa* and a hoe. At ten years of age, she should have had her own of both, but of course, she had not. Adwoa's hoe, she knew, was in the corner left of the door. She groped and found it. She also knew Adwoa's *apampa* was on the bamboo shelf. It was when she turned and was groping towards the bamboo shelf that she stumbled over the large water-bowl. Her chest hit the edge of the tray. The tray tilted and the water poured on the floor. She could not rise up. When Maami heard the noise her fall made, she screamed 'Thief! Thief! Thief! Everybody, come, there is a thief in my room.'

She gave the thief a chance to run away since he might attack her before the men of the village came. But no thief rushed through the door and there were no running footsteps in the courtyard. In fact, all was too quiet.

She picked up the lantern, pushed the wick up to blazing point and went gingerly to the outer room. There was Yaaba, sprawled like a freshly-killed overgrown cock on the tray. She screamed again.

'Ah Yaaba, why do you frighten me like this? What were you looking for? That is why I always say you are a witch. What do you want at this time of the night that you should fall on a water-bowl? And look at the floor. But of course, you were playing when someone lent me a piece of red earth to polish it, eh?' The figure in the tray just lay there. Maami bent down to help her up and then she saw the hoe. She stood up again.

'A hoe! I swear by all that be that I do not understand this.' She lifted her up and was carrying her to the inner room when Yaaba's lips parted as if to say something. She closed the lips again, her eyelids fluttered down and the neck sagged. 'My Saviour!' There was nothing strange in the fact that the cry was heard in the north and south of the village. Was it not past midnight?

People had heard Maami's first cry of 'Thief' and by the time she cried out again, the first men were coming from all directions. Soon the courtyard was full. Questions and answers went round. Some said Yaaba was trying to catch a thief, others that she was running from her mother's beating. But the first thing was to wake her up.

'Pour anowata into her nose!' – and the mothers ran into their husbands' chambers to bring their giant-sized bottles of the sweetest scents. 'Touch her feet with a little fire.' . . . 'Squeeze a little ginger juice into her nose.'

The latter was done and before she could suffer further ordeals, Yaaba's eyelids fluttered up.

'*Aa. . . . Oo* . . . we thank God. She is awake, she is awake.' Everyone said it. Some were too far away and saw her neither in the faint nor awake. But they said it as they trooped back to piece together their broken sleep. Egya Yaw, the village medicine-man, examined her and told the now-mad Maami that she should not worry. 'The impact was violent but I do not think anything has happened to the breast-bone. I will bind her up in beaten herbs and she should be all right in a few days.' 'Thank you, Egya,' said Maami, Paapa, her grandmother, the other mothers and all her relatives. The medicine-man went to his house and came back. Yaaba's brawniest uncles beat up the herbs. Soon, Yaaba was bound up. The cock had crowed once, when they laid her down. Her relatives then left for their own homes. Only Maami, Paapa and the other mothers were left. 'And how is she?' one of the women asked.

'But what really happened?'

'Only Benyiwa can answer you.'

'Benyiwa, what happened?'

'But I am surprised myself. After she had eaten her kenkey this afternoon, I heard her movements in the outer room but I did not mind her. Then she went away and came back when it was dark to eat her food. After our talk, I went to sleep. And there she was lying. As usual, she had not had a wash, so I just held her . . .'

'You held her what? Had she met with death you would

have been the one that pushed her into it – beating a child in the night!'

'But Yaaba is too troublesome!'

'And so you think every child will be good? But how did she come to fall in the tray?'

'That is what I cannot tell. My eyes were just playing me tricks when I heard some noise in the outer room.'

'Is that why you cried "Thief"?'

'Yes. When I went to see what it was, I saw her lying in the tray, clutching a hoe.'

'A hoe?'

'Yes, Adwoa's hoe.'

'Perhaps there was a thief after all? She can tell us the truth . . . but . . .'

So they went on through the early morning. Yaaba slept. The second cock-crow came. The church bell soon did its Christmas reveille. In the distance, they heard the songs of the dawn procession. Quite near in the doorway, the regular pat, pat of the twins' footsteps drew nearer towards the elderly group by the hearth. Both parties were surprised at the encounter.

'Children, what do you want at dawn?'

'Where is Yaaba?'

'Yaaba is asleep.'

'May we go and wake her, she asked us to.'

'Why?'

'She said she will go with us to the red-earth pit.'

'O . . . O!' The group around the hearth was amazed but they did not show it before the children.

'*Yoo*. You go today. She may come with you next time.'

'*Yoo*, Mother.'

'Walk well, my children. When she wakes up, we shall tell her you came.'

'We cannot understand it. Yaaba? What affected her head?'

'My sister, the world is a strange place. That is all.'

'And my sister, the child that will not do anything is better than a sheep.'

'Benyiwa, we will go and lie down a little.'

'Good morning.'

'Good morning.'

'Good morning.'

'*Yoo*. I thank you all.'

So Maami went into the apartment and closed the door. She knelt by the sleeping Yaaba and put her left hand on her bound chest. 'My child, I say thank you. You were getting ready to go and fetch me red earth? Is that why you were holding the hoe? My child, my child, I thank you.'

And the tears streamed down her face. Yaaba heard 'My child' from very far away. She opened her eyes. Maami was weeping and still calling her 'My child' and saying things which she did not understand.

Is Maami really calling me that? May the twins come. Am I Maami's own child?

'My child Yaaba . . .'

But how will I get red earth?

But why can I not speak . . .?

'I wish the twins would come . . .'

I want to wear the gold earrings . . .

I want to know whether Maami called me her child. Does it mean I am her child like Adwoa is? But one does not ask our elders such questions. And anyway, there is too much pain. And there are barriers where my chest is.

Probably tomorrow . . . but now Maami called me 'My child!' . . .

And she fell asleep again.

Something to Talk About on the Way to the Funeral

. . . Adwoa my sister, when did you come back?

'Last night.'

Did you come specially for Auntie Araba?

'What else, my sister? I just rushed into my room to pick up my *akatado* when I heard the news. How could I remain another hour in Tarkwa after getting such news? I arrived in the night.'

And your husband?

'He could not come. You know government-work. You must give notice several days ahead if you want to go away for half of one day. O, and so many other problems. But he will see to all that before next *Akwanbo*. Then we may both be present for the festival and the libation ceremony if her family plans it for a day around that time.'

Did you hear the Bosoë dance group practising the bread song?

'Yes. I hear they are going to make it the chief song at the funeral this afternoon. It is most fitting that they should do that. After all, when the group was formed, Auntie Araba's bread song was the first one they turned into a Bosoë song and danced to.'

Yes, it was a familiar song in those days. Indeed it had been heard around here for over twenty years. First in Auntie Araba's own voice with its delicate thin sweetness that clung like asawa berry on the tongue: which later, much later, had roughened a little. Then all of a sudden, it changed again, completely. Yes, it still was a woman's voice. But it was deeper and this time, like good honey, was rough and heavy, its sweetness within itself.

'Are you talking of when Mansa took over the hawking of the bread?'

Yes. That is how, in fact, that whole little quarter came to be known as *Bosohwe*. Very often, Auntie Araba did not have to carry the bread. The moment the aroma burst out of the oven, children began tugging at their parents' clothes for pennies and threepences. Certainly, the first batch was nearly always in those penny rows. Dozens of them. Of course, the children always caught the aroma before their mothers did.

'Were we not among them?'

We were, my sister. We remember that on market days and other holidays, Auntie Araba's ovenside became a little market-place all by itself. And then there was Auntie Araba herself. She always was a beautiful woman. Even three months ago when they were saying that all her life was gone, I thought she looked better than some of us who claim to be in our prime. If she was a young woman at this time when they are selling beauty to our big men in the towns, she would have made something for herself.

'Though it is a crying shame that young girls should be doing that. As for our big men! Hmm, let me shut my trouble-seeking mouth up. But our big men are something else too. You know, indeed, these our educated big men have never been up to much good.'

Like you know, my sister. After all, was it not a lawyer-or-a-doctor-or-something-like-that who was at the bottom of all Auntie Araba's troubles?

I did not know that, my sister.

Yes, my sister. One speaks of it only in whispers. Let me turn my head and look behind me. . . . And don't go standing in the river telling people. Or if you do, you better not say that you heard it from me.

115

'How could I do that? Am I a baby?'

Yes, Auntie Araba was always a beauty. My mother says she really was a come-and-have-a-look type, when she was a girl. Her plaits hung at the back of her neck like the branches of a giant tree, while the skin of her arms shone like charcoal from good wood. And since her family is one of these families with always some members abroad, when Auntie Araba was just about getting ready for her puberty, they sent her to go and stay at A— with some lady relative. That's where she learnt to mess around with flour so well. But after less than four years, they found she was in trouble.

'*Eh-eh?*'

Eh-eh, my sister. And now bring your ear nearer.

. . . .

'That lawyer-or-doctor-or-something-like-that who was the lady's husband?'

Yes.

'And what did they do about it?'

They did not want to spoil their marriage so they hushed up everything and sent her home quietly. Very quietly. That girl was our own Auntie Araba. And that child is Ato, the big scholar we hear of.

'*Ei*, there are plenty of things in the world's old box to pick up and talk about, my sister.'

You have said it. But be quiet and listen. I have not finished the story. If anything like that had happened to me, my life would have been ruined. Not that there is much to it now. But when Auntie Araba returned home to her mother, she was looking like a ram from the north. Big, beautiful and strong. And her mother did not behave as childishly as some would in a case like this. No, she did not tear herself apart as if the world had fallen down. . . .

'Look at how Mother Kuma treated her daughter. Rained insults on her head daily, refused to give her food and then drove her out of their house. Ah, and look at what the father of Mansa did to her too. . . .'

But isn't this what I am coming to? This is what I am coming to.

'Ah-h-h . . .'

Anyway, Auntie Araba's mother took her daughter in and treated her like an egg until the baby was born. And then did Auntie Araba tighten her girdle and get ready to work? Lord, there is no type of dough of flour they say she has not mixed and fried or baked. *Epitsi? Tatare? Atwemo? Bofrot? Boodo? Boodoo-ngo? Sweetbad? Hei*, she went there and dashed here. But they say that somehow, she was not getting much from these efforts. Some people even say that they landed her in debts.

'But I think someone should have told her that these things are good to eat but they suit more the tastes of the town-dwellers. I myself cannot see any man or woman who spends his living days on the farm, wasting his pennies on any of these sweeties which only satisfy the tongue but do not fill the stomach. Our people in the villages might buy *tatare* and *epitsi*, yes, but not the others.'

Like you know, my sister. This is what Auntie Araba discovered, but only after some time. I don't know who advised her to drop all those fancy foods. But she did, and finally started baking bread, ordinary bread. That turned out better for her.

'And how did she come to marry Egya Nyaako?'

They say that she grew in beauty and in strength after her baby was weaned. Good men and rich from all the villages of the state wanted to marry her.

'*Ei*, so soon? Were they prepared to take her with her baby?'

tartare – plantain pancake
epitsi – plantain cake
boodoo – sweet, unleavened corn bread
atwemo – plain sugared pastry drawn out in strips and fried in hot oil

boodoo-ngo – bread of unleavened corn meal mixed with palm oil and baked
bofrot – doughnuts
sweetbad – a hard coconut pastry baked or fried

117

Yes.

'Hmm, a good woman does not rot.'

That is what our fathers said.

'And she chose Egya Nyaako?'

Yes. But then, we should remember that he was a good man himself.

'Yes, he was. I used to be one of those he hired regularly during the cocoa harvests. He never insisted that we press down the cocoa as most of these farmers do. No, he never tried to cheat us out of our fair pay.'

Which is not what I can say of his heir!

'Not from what we've heard about him. A real mean one they say he is.'

So Auntie agreed to marry Egya Nyaako and she and her son came to live here. The boy, this big scholar we now know of, went with the other youngsters to the school the first day they started it here. In the old Wesleyan chapel. They say she used to say that if she never could sleep her fill, it was because she wanted to give her son a good education.

'*Poo*, pity. And that must have been true. She mixed and rolled her dough far into the night, and with the first cock-crow, got up from bed to light her fires. Except on Sundays.'

She certainly went to church twice every Sunday. She was a good Christian. And yet, look at how the boy turned out and what he did to her.

'Yes? You know I have been away much of the time. And I have never heard much of him to respect. Besides, I only know very little.'

That is the story I am telling you. I am taking you to bird-town so I can't understand why you insist on searching for eggs from the suburb!

'I will not interrupt you again, my sister.'

Maybe, it was because she never had any more children and therefore, Ato became an only child. They say she spoilt him. Though I am not sure I would not have done the same if I had been in her position. But they say that before he was six years old, he was fighting her. And he continued to fight her until he became a big scholar. And then his father came to acknowledge him as his son, and it seems that ruined him completely.

'Do you mean that lawyer-or-doctor-or-something-like-that man?'

Himself. They say he and his lady wife never had a male child so when he was finishing Stan' 7 or so, he came to father him.

'*Poo*, scholars!'

It is a shame, my sister. Just when all the big troubles were over.

'If I had been Auntie Araba, eh, I would have charged him about a thousand pounds for neglect.'

But Auntie Araba was not you. They say she was very happy that at last the boy was going to know his real father. She even hoped that that would settle his wild spirits. No, she did not want to make trouble. So this big man from the city came one day with his friends or relatives and met Auntie Araba and her relatives. It was one Sunday afternoon. In two big cars. They say some of her sisters and relatives had sharpened their mouths ready to give him what he deserved. But when they saw all the big men and their big cars, they kept quiet. They murmured among themselves, and that was all. He told them, I mean this new father, that he was going to send Ato to college.

'And did he?'

Yes he did. And he spoilt him even more than his mother had done. He gave him lots of money. I don't know what college he sent him to since I don't know about colleges. But he used to come here to spend some of his holidays. And every time, he left his mother with big debts to pay from his high living. Though I must add that she did not seem to mind.

'You know how mothers are, even when they have got several children.'

119

But, my sister, she really had a big blow when he put Mansa
into trouble. Mansa's father nearly killed her.

'I hear Mansa's father is a proud man who believes that
there is nothing which any man from his age group can do
which he cannot do better.'

So you know. When school education came here, all his children were too old to go to school except Mansa. And he used
to boast that he was only going to feel he had done his best
by her when she reached the biggest college in the white
man's land.

'And did he have the money?'

Don't ask me. As if I was in his pocket! Whether he had the
money or not, he was certainly saying these things. But then
people also knew him to add on these occasions, 'let us say
it will be good, so it shall be good'. Don't laugh, my sister.
Now, you can imagine how he felt when Ato did this to his
daughter Mansa. I remember they reported him as saying that
he was going to sue Ato for heavy damages. But luckily, Ato
just stopped coming here in the holidays. But of course, his
mother Auntie Araba was here. And she got something from
Mansa's father. And under his very nose was Mansa's own
mother. He used to go up and down ranting about some
women who had no sense to advise their sons to keep their
manhoods between their thighs, until they could afford the
consequences of letting them loose, and other mothers who
had not the courage to tie their daughters to their mats.

'O Lord.'

Yes, my sister.

'Hmm, I never knew any of these things.'

This is because you have been away in *the Mines* all the
time. But me, I have been here. I am one of those who sit in
that village waiting for the travellers. But also in connection
with this story, I have had the chance to know so much
because my husband's family house is in that quarter. I say,
Mansa's father never let anyone sleep. And so about the sixth
month of Mansa's pregnancy, her mother and Auntie Araba

decided to do something about the situation. Auntie Araba would take Mansa in, see her through until the baby was born and then later, they would think about what to do. So Mansa went to live with her. And from that moment, people did not even know how to describe the relationship between the two. Some people said they were like mother and daughter. Others that they were like sisters. Still more others even said they were like friends. When the baby was born, Auntie Araba took one or two of her relatives with her to Mansa's parents. Their purpose was simple. Mansa had returned from the battlefield safe. The baby looked strong and sound. If Mansa's father wanted her to go back to school . . .

'Yes, some girls do this.'

But Mansa's father had lost interest in Mansa's education. 'I can understand him.'

I too. So Auntie Araba said that in that case, there was no problem. Mansa was a good girl. Not like one of these *yetse-yetse* things who think putting a toe in a classroom turns them into goddesses. The child and mother should go on living with her until Ato finished his education. Then they could marry properly.

'Our Auntie Araba is going to heaven.'

If there is any heaven and God is not like man, my sister.

'What did Mansa's parents say?'

What else could they say? Her mother was very happy. She knew that if Mansa came back to live with them she would always remind her father of everything and then there would never be peace for anybody in the house. They say that from that time, the baking business grew and grew and grew. Mansa's hands pulled in money like a good hunter's gun does with game. Auntie Araba herself became young again. She used to say that if all mothers knew they would get daughters-in-law like Mansa, birth pains would be easier to bear. When her husband Egya Nyaako died, would she not have gone mad if Mansa was not with her? She was afraid of the time when her son would finish college, come and marry Mansa

121

properly and take her away. Three years later, Ato finished college. He is a teacher, as you know, my sister. The government was sending him to teach somewhere far away from here. Then about two weeks or so before Christmas, they got a letter from him that he was coming home.

'Ah, I am sure Mansa was very glad.'

Don't say it loudly, my sister. The news spread very fast. We teased her. 'These days some women go round with a smile playing round their lips all the time. Maybe there is a bird on the neem tree behind their back door which is giving them special good news,' we said. Auntie Araba told her friends that her day of doom was coming upon her. What was she going to do on her own? But her friends knew that she was also very glad. So far, she had looked after her charges very well. But if you boil anything for too long, it burns. Her real glory would come only when her son came to take away his bride and his child.

'And the boy-child was a very handsome somebody too.'

And clever, my sister. Before he was two, he was delighting us all by imitating his grandmother and his mother singing the bread-hawking song. A week before the Saturday Ato was expected, Mansa moved back to her parents' house.

'That was a good thing to do.'

She could not have been better advised. That Saturday, people saw her at her bath quite early. My little girl had caught a fever and I myself had not gone to the farm. When eleven o'clock struck, I met Mansa in the market-place, looking like a festive dish. I asked her if what we had heard was true, that our lord and master was coming on the market-day lorry that afternoon. She said I had heard right.

'Maybe she was very eager to see him and could not wait in the house.'

Could you have waited quietly if you had been her?

'Oh, women. We are to be pitied.'

Tell me, my sister. I had wanted to put a stick under the story and clear it all for you. But we are already in town.

'Yes, look at that crowd. Is Auntie Araba's family house near the mouth of this road?'

Oh yes. Until the town grew to the big thing it is, the Twidan Abusia house was right on the road but now it is behind about four or so other houses. Why?

'I think I can hear singing.'

Yes, you are right.

'She is going to get a good funeral.'

That, my sister, is an answer to a question no one will ask.

'So finish me the story.'

Hmm, kinsman, when the market lorry arrived, there was no Scholar-Teacher-Ato on it.

'No?'

No.

'What did Auntie Araba and Mansa do?'

What could they do? Everyone said that the road always has stories to tell. Perhaps he had only missed the lorry. Perhaps he had fallen ill just on that day or a day or so before. They would wait for a while. Perhaps he would arrive that evening if he thought he could get another lorry, it being a market day. But he did not come any time that Saturday or the next morning. And no one saw him on Monday or Tuesday.

'Ohhh . . .'

They don't say, ohhh. . . . We heard about the middle of the next week – I have forgotten now whether it was the Wednesday or Thursday – that he had come.

'*Eheh?*'

Nyo. But he brought some news with him. He could not marry Mansa.

'Oh, why? After spoiling her . . .'

If you don't shut up, I will stop.

'Forgive me and go on, my sister.'

Let us stand in this alley here – that is the funeral parlour over there. I don't want anyone to overhear us.

'You are right.'

Chicha Ato said he could not marry Mansa because he had got another girl into trouble.

'*Whopei!*'

She had been in the college too. Her mother is a big lady and her father is a big man. They said if he did not marry their daughter, they would finish him. . . .

'*Whopei!*'

His lawyer-father thought it advisable for him to wed that girl soon because they were afraid of what the girl's father would do.

'*Whopei!*'

So he could not marry our Mansa.

'*Whopei!*'

They don't say, *Whopei*, my sister.

'So what did they do?'

Who?

'Everybody. Mansa? Auntie Araba?'

What could they do?

'*Whopei!*'

That was just before you came back to have your third baby, I think.

'About three years ago?'

Yes.

'It was my fourth. I had the third in Aboso but it died.'

Then it was your fourth. Yes, it was just before you came.

'I thought Auntie Araba was not looking like herself. But I had enough troubles of my own and had no eyes to go prying into other people's affairs. . . . So that was that. . . .'

Yes. From then on, Auntie Araba was just lost.

'And Mansa-ah?'

She really is like Auntie herself. She has all of her character. She too is a good woman. If she had stayed here, I am sure someone else would have married her. But she left.

'And the child?'

She left him with her mother. Haven't you seen him since you came?

'No. Because it will not occur to anybody to point him out to me until I ask. And I cannot recognise him from my mind. I do not know him at all.'

He is around, with the other schoolchildren.

'So what does Mansa do?'

When she left, everyone said she would become a whore in the city.

'*Whopei.* People are bad.'

Yes. But perhaps they would have been right if Mansa had not been the Mansa we all know. We hear Auntie Araba sent her to a friend and she found her a job with some people. They bake hundreds of loaves of bread an hour with machines.

'A good person does not rot.'

No. She sent money and other things home.

'May God bless her. And Auntie Araba herself?'

As I was telling you. After this affair, she never became herself again. She stopped baking. Immediately. She told her friends that she felt old age was coming on her. Then a few months later, they say she started getting some very bad stomach aches. She tried here, she tried there. Hospitals first, then our own doctors and their herbs. Nothing did any good.

'O our end! Couldn't the hospital doctors cut her up and find out?'

My sister, they say they don't work like that. They have to find out what is wrong before they cut people up.

'And they could not find out what was wrong with Auntie Araba?'

No. She spent whatever she had on this stomach. Egya Nyaako, as you know, had already died. So, about three months ago, she packed up all she had and came here, to squat by her ancestral hearth.

'And yesterday afternoon she died?'

Yes, and yesterday afternoon she died.

'Her spirit was gone.'

Certainly it was her son who drove it away. And then Mansa left with her soul.

'Have you ever seen Chicha Ato's lady-wife?'

No. We hear they had a church wedding. But Auntie Araba did not put her feet there. And he never brought her to Ofuntumase.

'Maybe the two of them may come here today?'

I don't see how he can fail to come. But she, I don't know. Some of these ladies will not set foot in a place like this for fear of getting dirty.

'Hmmm . . . it is their own cassava! But do you think Mansa will come and wail for Auntie Araba?'

My sister, if you have come, do you think Mansa will not?

Other Versions

The whole thing had started after the school certificate exams. Instead of going straight home, I had stayed in town to work. This was going to be my first proper meeting with the town and when I sent the letter home announcing my intentions, I felt a little strange. Bekoe and I were going to stay in a small room in his uncle's house. The room was like a coffin but who cared? We found a job as sorting hands in the Post Office. I've forgotten how much they were paying us. Really it's strange . . . but I have. Anyway, it was something like twelve pounds. Either it started at fourteen pounds and then with the deductions leaned out to twelve-'n'-something or it was twelve with no taxes. But I remember twelve. Bekoe told me that his uncle was not expecting us to pay anything for the room and that he had even instructed his wife to give us three meals a day for free. I say, this was very kind of him. Because you know what? Some people would have insisted on our paying. They would have said it would help us get experienced at budgeting in the future. And in fact we later discovered that the wife didn't have it in mind to feed us free like that. After the first week, she hinted it would be nice if we considered contributing something. She was not charging us for the meals. No, she was just asking us to contribute something. We agreed on three pounds each. We also thought Bekoe shouldn't tell his uncle this. Not that Bekoe would have told on her anyway. He knew nephews and nieces have been able to break up marriages. *Ei*, he didn't want any trouble. Besides his mother would have killed him for it. His mother is a fierce trader and I know her. She could easily have slapped him and later boasted it around the market how she had beaten up her son who was finishing five years in college!

Anyhow, that was three pounds off the pay. Then there was this business of the blazer. I mean the school blazer I wanted to buy. It cost ten pounds and Father had made it quite clear that he considered his duty by me done when he paid my fees for the last term. How could I go to him with a blazer case? So I thought I would keep four pounds by every month towards that. We were going to work for three months. That was the only time we could have in the long vacation. You see, we both wanted to go to the sixth form. Well, if I was able to set by this four pounds every month, I would have two pounds over after I had bought it. And I could use this to look after myself until our pocket money from the government came.

Then I remembered what Mother had told me. I remembered her telling me one day that any time I got my first pay, I was to take something home. Part of this would be used to buy gin to pour libation to the spirits of our forefathers so they would come and bless me with prosperity. That was why the first Saturday after pay-day, I went to the lorry park and took *The Tailless Animal*. As for that lorry, *eh!* I was not surprised to read in Araba's letter the other day that Anan, its owner and driver, has bought a bus. Anyone would, after the two of them had for years literally owned what was to their right and to their left in the way of passengers.

Of course, I had always thought this money would go to Mother. And so see, how do you think I felt when, in a private discussion with her the afternoon I arrived, she told me it would be better if I gave it to Father? I had decided on four pounds here, too, reserving the last pound for regular spending. Anyway, the moment the money fell into her hand she burst into tears.

'*Ao*, I too am coming to something in this world. Who would have thought it? I never slept to dream that I shall live to see a day like this. . . . Now I too have got my own man who will take care of me. . . .' You know how women carry on when they mean to? She even knelt down to say a prayer of thanks to God and at that point I left the room. Yes, and after all this business she didn't take the silly money.

'Hand it over to your father. He will certainly buy a bottle of gin and pour some to the ancestors. Then I will ask him to give me about ten shillings to buy some yam and eggs for Sunday. . . .'

'That should leave at least three clear pounds,' I thought aloud.

'Listen my master, does it matter if your father has three pounds of your pay? It does not matter, I am telling you. Because then they shall not be able to say you have not given him anything since you started working.'

'But Mother, I am not starting work permanently.'

'And what do you mean?'

'Mother, I have done an examination. If I pass very well, I shall go to school again.'

'Ah, and were you not the one who made me understand that you would finish after five years?'

'Yes, but the government asks those who do very well to continue.'

'And does the government pay their fees too?'

'Yes.'

'Then that is good because I do not think your father would like to pay any more fees for you. Anyway, it does not matter about the money. You give it to him. His people do not know all these things about the government asking you to continue. What they know is that you are working.'

God!

I hadn't thought of giving anything of that sort. Certainly not that soon. . . . However, Sunday came and I ate the *oto* mother prepared with the yam and palm oil. I ate it with some

of the eggs to congratulate my soul. Then I went to say good-
bye to people, and Mother took me up to the mouth of the
road. Being a Sunday, we thought it would be useless to wait
for *The Tailless Animal* to wander in. Because it simply
wouldn't. It did that only on the weekdays.

And I was to realise that I hadn't heard the last of the money
business. Mother thought it would be good if I continued to
give that 'little something' to Father as long as I worked.

'*Ho*, Father?'

'Yes. You know he has done very well. Taking you through
college. Now, giving him something would not only show
your gratitude but also go towards your sisters' fees.'

Ei, I say, have you heard a story like this before? I tell you,
eh, I caught a fever in the raw. But Mother was still talking.

'I had thought of a nice dignified something like five
pounds. But you brought four this time and maybe it will be
better to maintain just that.'

'And how much do I give you?'

'Me?' She sounded quite shocked – 'why should you bring
me anything? I do not need your money. All I want is for you
to be happy and you shall not be if they say you are bad. And
do you think I am an old fool to ask you for money? If you
give that to your father, you will be doing a lot. Say you will
do it, Kofi.'

'I shall do it, Mother,' I parroted.

I had a dazed feeling for the rest of the journey and the
whole day. I just could not figure it out. To begin with, whose
child was I? Why should I have to pay my father for sending
me to school? And calling that 'college' did not help me either.
Besides he only paid half the fees, since the Cocoa Brokers'
Union, of which he is a member, had given me a scholarship
to cover the other half. And anyway, Father. He is the kind of
parent who checks out lists so thoroughly you would think
his life depends upon them. And he doesn't mind which kind
either. Textbook lists? '*Hei*, didn't I buy you a dictionary
last year?' The lists of provisions you needed to survive the

near-starvation diet in a boarding school? 'And whom are you going to feed with a dozen Heinz baked beans?'

Well, you know them. In fact from talking to people you learn that most fathers are like that and that's the only nice thing about it. Anyway Father is surely like that. It was a battle he and I fought at the beginning of every term. Once when Mother didn't know I was within earshot I heard her telling my little aunt that Father always feels through his coins for the ones which have gone soft to give away! Don't laugh. It's not very funny when you are his son. So you see why I got so mad to have Mother talk to me in that way? And the main thing was, it wasn't the money I was giving away which hurt me. It was the idea of Father getting it. I had always thought of making a small allowance for Mother from the moment I started working. I was the third child. My two older brothers were all working but married and couldn't care much about the rest of us. There were two girls after me, then one other boy. Father pays the fees and complains all the time. Mother gets us clothes and feeds us too because the three pounds he gives for our chop-money is a nice joke. Mother peddles cloth but I know she is not the fat rich market type – say, like Bekoe's mother. In the villages you always have to settle for instalments and money comes in in such miserable bits someone like Mother with four children just spends every penny of her profit as it comes. It is her favourite saying that she sells cloth for the fish-and-cassava women. There is always a threat of her eating into her capital. And naturally, it was of her I had thought in terms of any money-giving I was going to do.

But I obeyed her. I sent four pounds to Father at the end of the remaining months and each time just about burst up. 'Why not Mother? Why not Mother?' I kept asking myself. It drove me wild.

Well, we went to the sixth form. And of course Father realised I was still in school. He was quite proud of me too. He always managed to let slip into conversations with other men how Kofi was planning to go to the Unifartisy. Oh, it was fine as long as he was not paying. . . .

I passed higher and with lots of distinctions. I stopped working at my holiday jobs to get ready to go to our national University. And then I met Mr. Buntyne, who had been our chemistry teacher. He asked me if I would be interested in a scholarship for an American University. He knew a business syndicate. They were looking out for especially bright young people to help. They had not had an African yet. But he was sure they would be interested. Of course I applied. There were endless forms to fill out but I got the scholarship. And I came here.

Somehow I never forgot the money for Mother. I told myself that I would do something about that the first thing after graduation. Perhaps it is the way she genuinely thinks she does not need my earnings that much which makes me want to do something for her. I've even thought of finding a vacation job here to do so I can send some of my pay home with express instructions that it is for her. But that I know will distress her no end. Better still, I planned to save as much money as I could so I could take her about forty pounds or even four hundred to do something with. Like building a house 'for you children' as she always put it. . . .

And then somehow this thing happened. It was the very first month I came. I was invited by Mr. Merrows to go and have dinner with him and his family. He is either the chairman of this syndicate which brought me here or certainly one of its top men. They came to pick me up from the campus to their house. Oh, to be sure, it was a high and mighty hut. Everything was perfect. There were other guests besides the Merrows family. The food was gorgeous but the main course for the evening was me. What did I think of America? How did I plan to use this unique opportunity in the service of Africa? How many wives did my father have? etc., etc., etc.

I had assumed that everyone in the household was there at the dinner table. Mrs. Merrows kept popping in and out of the kitchen serving the food. And as I've said before, the food was really very good. Everyone complimented her on it and she smiled and gave the wives the recipes for this and that.

A couple of hours after the meal, Mr. Merrows proposed to take me back to the campus because it was getting late. I agreed. I said my thanks and good-nights and followed Mr. Merrows to the door. I waited for him while he pulled out the car from the garage. He asked me to jump in and I did. But then he left his seat, leaving the engine running and returned some five or ten minutes later followed by someone. It turned out to be a black woman. You know what sometimes your heart does? Mine did that just then. Kind of turned itself round in a funny way. Mr. Merrows opened the back seat for her and said,

'Kofi, Mrs. Hye helps us with the cooking sometimes and since I am taking you back anyway, I thought I could take her at least half her way. Mrs. Hye, Kofi is from Africa.'

In the car she and I smiled nervously at each other. . . . I tried not to feel agitated.

But then was it the next evening or two? I don't even remember.

I was returning again to the campus from visiting a boy I knew back at home and whom I had met the first few days I arrived. I took the subway. When the train pulled up at the station, I got into the car nearest to me. It looked empty. I sat down. Then I raised my eyes and realised there was someone else in it. There was a black woman sitting to the left end of the opposite seat.

Another black woman.

Now I can't tell whether she really was old or just middle-aged. She certainly was not young. I realised I had to be careful or I would be staring. She was just normal black with a buttony mouth, pretty deep-set eyes and an old black hand-bag. Somehow I noticed the bag. She was wearing the lined raincoat affair which everyone wears around here in the autumn. Except that I felt hers was too thin for that time of night.

That time of night.

I got to thinking of what a woman her age would be wanting in a subway car that time of night. I don't know why but immediately I remembered the other one who had been in the Merrows' kitchen while they ate and I ate. Then I started getting confused. I can swear the woman knew I was trying not to stare. She most probably knew too that I was thinking about her. Anyway, I don't know what made me. But I drew out my wallet. I had received money from my scholarship. So I took some dollar bills, crumpled them in my hand and jumped like one goaded with a firebrand.

'Eh . . . eh . . . I come from Africa and you remind me of my mother. Please would you take this from me?'

And all the time, I was trying hard not to stare.

'Sit down,' she said.

I'm not sure I really heard these words above the din. But I know she patted the space by her. The train was pulling up at a station.

'You say you come from Africa?' she said.

'Yes,' I said.

'What are you doing here, son?' she asked.

'A student,' I replied shortly.

'Son, keep them dollars. I sure know you need them more than I do,' she said. Of course, she was Mother. And so there was no need to see. But now I could openly look at her beautiful face. I got out at the stop. She waved to me and smiled. I stood there on the platform until the engine had wheezed and raged out of sight. I looked at the money which was still in my hand. I felt like opening them out; I did. There was one ten-dollar bill and two single ones. Twelve dollars. Then it occurred to me that that was as near to four pounds as you could get. It was not a constriction in the throat. Rather, the dazed feeling I had had that Sunday afternoon on the high road to town came back. And as I stumbled through the exit, and up the stairs, I heard myself mutter, 'O Mother.'

Telling Stories and Transforming Postcolonial Society

Ketu H. Katrak

Storytelling, History, Kinship

> I come from a people who told stories. . . . My mother
> 'talks' stories and sings songs. . . . [She] is definitely a
> direct antecedent. Having my daughter Kinna has also
> influenced my writing. . . . My mother has been a tower of
> strength (Interview with Aidoo; James 1990, 19–20).

Ama Ata Aidoo's work as creative artist, cultural worker,
teacher, and thinker makes significant contributions to African
literature and culture. Her diverse literary achievements in
drama, poetry, fiction, and essays illuminate struggles and triumphs facing women and men in their post-independence
Ghanaian society. Aidoo is a creative writer who believes
ardently that telling stories and reciting poems can inspire
social change. Her vision is historic, committed to black peoples
in Africa and the diaspora, as well as feminist. Aidoo casts a
probing though sympathetic eye on colonial history and postcolonial realities, on her people's ancient traditions and the
dubious paradoxes of modernization. Her work represents
how the personal and the intimate are as political as public discussions of law and nation. "Even in terms of the relationship
between a man and a woman," she remarks, "the factors that
affect the relationship are very often outside of themselves;

135

they have to do with social structure, with economics, with political reality" (Modebe 1991, 40).

Aidoo's artistic and social commitments unfold seamlessly and are rooted in her personal family history. Christened Christina Ama Ata Aidoo, she was born on March 23, 1942, in Abeadzi Kyiakor in Ghana's central region. Aidoo acknowledges that her mother shared a rich heritage of "talking" stories with her daughter. She first "heard" what later became *Anowa,* a drama, in the form of a song that her mother sang. "Looking back to my parentage," Aidoo remarks, "I think I come from a long line of fighters.... I have always been interested in the destiny of our people.... I am one of these writers whose writings cannot move too far from their political involvement" (James 1990, 13–14). Her paternal grandfather was "tortured to death in a colonial prison for being 'an insolent African'"; and her father supported Kwame Nkrumah and believed that, "`above all, a nation should educate its women'" (quoted in Allan 1993, 191). Aidoo had first heard Dr. Kwegyir Aggrey's famous statement from her father, "If you educate a man, you educate an individual. If you educate a woman, you educate a nation." Her father was very keen that Aidoo receive an education "in spite of the prevailing bias," notes Allan, "against schooling for girls" (192). Aidoo attended the Wesley Girls' High School at Cape Coast where her writerly bent was encouraged by an English teacher, Barbara Bowman, whose gift of an Olivetti typewriter was most valuable to the aspiring young writer.

Aidoo's first published story, "To Us a Child Is Born," won a Christmas story competition in 1958, when she was sixteen. Her second story, "No Sweetness Here," brought her an invitation four years later to the historic 1962 African Writers' Workshop held at the University of Ibadan, Nigeria. Aidoo was quite overwhelmed, introduced as "the writer from Ghana" (as she remarked at a recent African Writers' Conference at Brown University). Here she met several famous male writers—Chinua Achebe, Wole Soyinka,

Christopher Okigbo. Aidoo returned to Ghana and wrote *The Dilemma of a Ghost*, which was produced in 1964 at the University of Ghana and published in 1965. Her consciousness of black history, of the cultural and historical links among black peoples in the diaspora, motivated this remarkable first drama which placed Aidoo at age twenty-three among the new generation of predominantly male African writers. The historical link between Africans and African Americans that Aidoo explores in this early drama was guided by her astute political vision of black peoples in the diaspora. From this first work, and through all subsequent work, Aidoo claims "a responsibility and I feel that it's the same type of responsibility I think black people all over feel" (quoted in Pieterse and Duerden 1972, 20).

The Dilemma of a Ghost presents African-American Eulalie Rush, who marries Ghanaian Ato Yawson and returns to her "roots" in Africa. In 1964 such pride in African ancestry, in blackness, and in the discovery of African antecedents in African-American culture, were new concepts in the United States. Even at this early stage, Aidoo recognized that "the whole question of how it was that so many of our people could be enslaved and sold is very very important. I've always thought that it is an area that must be probed. It probably holds one of the keys to our future" (James 1990, 20–21). In her formative years in her parents' progressive home, and in Nkrumah's Ghana, awareness about connections among black people in the diaspora were not unusual. "Maybe it is because," she remarks, "I come from a people from whom, for some reason, the connection with African-America or the Caribbean was a living thing, something of which we were always aware. In Nkrumah's Ghana one met African Americans and people from the Caribbean. In my father's house we were always getting visitors from all over" (James 1990, 20).

Aidoo graduated from the University of Ghana in 1964 and then attended a creative writing program at Stanford

University. She was married and has one daughter. "Being a mother," remarks Aidoo, "has been a singularly enriching experience" (James 1990, 13). As a writer and a teacher, she has worked in numerous university settings. In 1968 and 1969 she taught in the School of Drama of the University of Dar es Salaam, Tanzania, and in the English department of the University of Nairobi in Kenya. She worked as coordinator of the African literature program at Cape Coast from 1972 to 1982. More recently, she has been a writer-in-residence or visiting professor at the University of Richmond, Virginia, Oberlin College, and Brandeis University.

In Ghana, Allan notes, "from 1972 to 1979, Aidoo held directorships at the Ghana Broadcasting Corporation, the Arts Council of Ghana, and the Medical and Dental Council. This period of social activism culminated in her appointment as Minister of Education in 1982"(193). Aidoo took that post because, as she remarks in her interview with James, "I believe that education is the key to everything. Whereas I do not discount my work as a writer or the possibility of doing things with my writing, I thought that out there as minister, or whatever, you have a direct access to state power, to affect things and to direct them immediately . . . but . . . you can't do that on your own, you are linked to other forces" (11). Aidoo recognized that the entire educational "structure needed shaking up, revolutionizing" (Modebe 1991, 40).

After a year as minister of education, and because she wanted uninterrupted time to work on her writing, she left Ghana for Zimbabwe. But Aidoo always divides her time among teaching, writing, and activist work. Hence, even as she worked on her novel *Changes* (published in 1991 in Britain and in 1993 in the United States), she worked with "the Zimbabwean Women Writers' Union, the Ministry of Education, and women's tie-dye groups," activities which demonstrate that "Aidoo remains steeped," remarks Allan, "in African cultural life" (193).

Urbanization in Post-Independence Ghana

My Brother,
let's just have
—another cup of tea—

And if
this is
the
neo-colonial crime
ask for
whose art it was

Before the British
stole
it.

(*Someone Talking to Sometime,* 25)

All of Aidoo's creative concerns deal with Ghanaian society. Ghana, formerly known as the Gold Coast, was the first
African colony to gain independence from the British in 1957.
Nationalism and anticolonial struggles led to independence,
and sadly to what Neil Lazarus terms "the mourning after"
(Lazarus 1990, 1). Given the historical onslaught of colonialism and the neocolonialism and imperialism that continues
today, Ghana, like other postcolonial nations of West Africa, is
caught in a long and unhappy transition. Colonial rule introduced a capitalist wage-economy, English law, English language, and English mores where quite different cultural realities existed.[1] The colonial interruption of Africa's history was
a violent one—not only in terms of economic plunder, but in
the far more devastating and lingering impact of psychological colonization that persisted long after the so-called depar-
ture of colonial masters.[2]

Afterword

Aidoo's vision of this history governs all her work. In her two early dramas, *The Dilemma of a Ghost* (1965) and *Anowa* (1970), she spans vast time periods and geographies to describe slavery and colonization. Evocative and dramatic artistic works, these plays boldly raise issues of Europe's accountability for "underdeveloping Africa," to use Walter Rodney's phrase.

One of the major social effects of colonization was urbanization. *No Sweetness Here*, first published in 1970, is especially sensitive to problems resulting from the shift of rural people to urban centers, the accompanying loss of traditional mores, and the transition to modern ways. Aidoo's complex vision also recognizes that the notion of "transition" can be a cop-out—a society can be transitioning endlessly.[3] In these stories, Aidoo does not escape into easy binary oppositions: tradition/modernity, rural/urban. Rather, she probes the places in which these postcolonial conditions overlap and intersect. Her work traverses the geographies of rural farming environments and urban, skylined landscapes, as these locations are often co-inhabited by her characters. Even as "city folk," they come from rural origins. Often through astute uses of irony, wit, and humor, Aidoo renders both nurturing and destructive collisions when rural folk enter cities and vice versa.

Similarly, Aidoo views modernization as multifaceted, and not necessarily beneficial. Modernization often functions as a sword that the colonizer wields by its handle, leaving the colonized to grasp the blade. One icon of modernization is the building of roads that link villages to cities, and as readers we travel extensively with Aidoo's characters—from the north of Ghana to the south, from a village near Cape Coast into the city. Aidoo's dramatic narratives put us as readers on a lorry, breathing the fumes, feeling the road as experienced by an elderly woman undertaking this journey for the first time in her life. The external journeys mirror the interior landscapes of the characters entering new regions geographically and mentally in the alienating world of the city.

While there are no white characters in *No Sweetness Here*,

140

colonialism exists as part of internalized mentalities, psychological and economic burdens left behind by Europeans. Whiteness is most clearly a psychological burden for the educated class, schooled in the English language and Western classics. It is an ironic reality of the postcolonial condition (as depicted also by other postcolonial writers such as Zimbabwean Tsitsi Dangarembga in her novel *Nervous Conditions*) that this educated class is simultaneously privileged and disadvantaged. It can abuse its privileges as the "big men" in Aidoo's stories do by sexually using young women, or as corrupt politicians who exploit the nation. This educated class is disadvantaged in that it is often caught in conflicts between traditional ways and more modern values that challenge certain restrictive aspects of tradition. This type of dilemma faces educated women doubly, since they can be ostracized further from their communities for challenging the patriarchal status quo.

The Oral Tradition

> We cannot assume that all literature should be written. One doesn't have to be so patronizing about oral literature.... The art of the speaking voice can be brought back so easily.... We don't always have to write for readers, we can write for listeners (Aidoo in Pieterse and Duerden 1972, 23–24).

Aidoo passionately believes in "oral narration as an artistic mode" (James 1990, 23). Although she belongs among African and postcolonial writers who speak their own mother tongues but who use the English language for their creative work—a legacy of British colonization—she believes that "the dynamism of orality" is what "Africa can give to the world" (James 1990, 23).[4]

While African literature in English can be dated to when most African nations became independent in the 1960s, the recentness of these English-language traditions must be distinguished from the much older cultural heritages, often oral, of the African continent. Many precolonial African cultures, predominantly oral, lost ancient oral literary traditions rendered invisible by racism and a Western belief in the superiority of written language and literature. Along with such erasure of language went devastating denials of culture and identity.

Unlike most women writers, who are comfortable with the novel form, Aidoo is happiest with drama, perhaps because the dramatic form with heard voices, dialogue, and audience participation links her most closely to orality:

> Probably I am unhappiest with the novel simply because it is too many words. I think that once my uncertainties with poetry as a form and its accessibility have been resolved, what I mean, if I wasn't so busy worrying about poetry not being accessible, I am very happy with poetry. But I am happiest of all with drama. Given some other circumstances I would have liked to write more plays. (James 1990, 22)

Aidoo's short stories are remarkable for her uses of orality. Aidoo's unique form of oral textuality guides and governs the thematic exploration of sociocultural, gender, and political issues facing postcolonial Ghanaian society. Even as Aidoo's plays "capitalize," as Lloyd Brown puts it, "on the dramatic art of storytelling," her integration of the narrative and the dramatic are noteworthy in her short stories (Brown 1981, 84).

Aidoo recognizes the all-inclusiveness of the oral storyteller's artistry, combining dramatic representation, plot, character, and suspense. Moreover, as Brown rightly notes, "This art is social in the most literal sense." The artist/narrator is present before his/her audience, and "the story itself reflects and perpetuates the moral and cultural values of the audience" (84).

Aidoo's rootedness in Akan oral traditions and folk forms

serves her creativity in experimenting insightfully with, and in mixing, literary forms of prose, poetry, and drama in her short stories. There are no rigid boundaries in oral traditions, which flow optimally from prose, into poetry, into narrative, into dramatic interlude, into song. Aidoo creatively transmutes several characteristics of orality—conversing with the listeners, audience participation, communal voices as chorus, dramatic dialogue, repetition—into written, "heard" texts, her own dynamic form of oral textuality. The stories can be performed as dramatic readings with one narrator taking on different character roles, or with several readers playing different characters. As in drama, characters appear in Aidoo's stories fully formed, at times without names, at times playing the role of communal, choral commentators, at other times, engaged in a lively discussion of some dilemma facing society. For instance, Aidoo opens "The Message" with a striking medley of voices discussing, dialoguing, repeating, and trying to figure out exactly what has been conveyed to Maami Amfoa in "this tengram [telegram] thing":

> 'Look here my sister, it should not be said but they
> say they opened her up.'
> 'They opened her up?'
> 'Yes, opened her up.'
> 'And the baby removed?'
> 'Yes, the baby removed.'
> 'Yes, the baby removed.'
> 'I say . . . '
> 'They do not say, my sister.'
> 'Have you heard it?'
> 'What?'
> 'This and this and that . . . '
> 'A-a-ah! that is it . . . ' (38)

Aidoo does not name these communal voices; their identities are conveyed in their anxious voices as they introduce the story before we meet Maami Amfoa. The suspense builds up almost to the end of the tale when we are relieved to learn that Maami's only granddaughter has survived, giving birth to twins by cesarean section.

Orality is conveyed also by Aidoo's representation of communal voices, where she deliberately leaves the speakers' identities unspecified. She then skillfully intersperses Maami's own thoughts, often her unspoken fears, as in the line, "My Lord, hold me tight. . . ." Maami is so terrified in this alien space called hospital that she cannot even speak.

Even as Aidoo's ear recreates the voices of recited tales, she draws distinctively upon the oral tradition of the dilemma tale for her dramas and short stories as she probes problems facing society. According to Brown, the dilemma tale "usually poses difficult questions of moral or legal significance. These questions are usually debated both by the narrator and the audience—and on this basis the dilemma is a good example of the highly functional nature of oral art in traditional Africa" (85). William Bascom comments on his study of dilemma tales from the Akan region in Ghana: "They are prose narratives that leave the listeners with a choice among alternatives. . . . The choices are difficult ones and usually involve discrimination on ethical, moral, or legal grounds." Bascom further notes that these tales additionally function to train the listeners "in the skills of argumentation and debate," useful in settling disputes within the home or in courts of law (quoted in Brown 1981, 85). The dilemma tale often poses unanswerable questions or provokes debates that "really function," notes Brown, "as a kind of intellectual exercise that develops and continually stimulates the audience's ability to discuss such dilemmas in everyday existence" (85–86).

Dilemmas of Modernity: Through the Prisms of Colonialism, Independence, and Postcolonialism

The eleven stories of *No Sweetness Here* explore several dilemmas that resonate differently for women and men, for the very young, the elderly, and those in the middle of their lives—the latter perhaps caught most painfully in a society moving from traditional values to modern ways.

The opening and closing narratives where the West is insidiously and pervasively present in terms of racism, economic exploitation, and psychological colonization provide a frame for *No Sweetness Here*. In the initial and concluding stories of the collection, Western-educated Africans returning home or living abroad are the focus. Through their confused eyes, the dilemmas are sharpened for the readers. Several major dilemmas appear in Aidoo's stories that probe forthrightly, and often with wit and humor, post-independence disillusionment and confusion of gender roles as they relate to race and class, the ambivalence of modernization as "progress," and conflicts in gender and kinship roles in newly developed urban areas, particularly in women's limited work options in cities. The dilemmas of the ascendancy of Western-educated "big men"—corrupt politicians who exploit the nation and young women—are also explored, as are women's trials as mothers, prostitutes, and wives. For example, in "For Whom Things Did Not Change," Zirigu faces post-independence disillusionment at the new black ruling class that did not consider him deserving of modern amenities like electricity and a good lavatory. The same story also probes the dilemmas of changing gender roles as they relate to race and class. Profound differences of class and education override racial commonality between the black, Western-educated Kobina and the black Zirigu as the older man addresses the younger as "My White Massa!" Zirigu expects Kobina to eat "white man chop," as is the norm for white and black masters of Kobina's class (16).

145

While Zirigu is adept at cooking white peoples' food—that is his job—he is horrified by Kobina's request for local food. Cooking local food is woman's work!

Differences between the two men are embodied in Aidoo's uses of language in this story—Zirigu uses broken pidgin English when he speaks as servant to his master Kobina, but standard English when communicating as an equal (even as a superior in terms of his male privilege) when talking to his wife. Aidoo subtly criticizes Kobina's well-intentioned, though naive, desire to effect overnight a radical transformation of class and education barriers and hierarchies between Zirigu and himself. Unfortunately, in reality, the social change from white masters to black masters leaves everything else intact. Class and education rather than race, then, govern social relations. Most new black masters expect the same servility from Zirigu that he had shown to the white colonial masters. This black bourgeois class has moved beyond the traditional value of showing respect for elders.

Another modern dilemma, "big men" abusing and sexualizing women by luring them with new, flashy cars and new, flashy salaries, also comes under Aidoo's severe invective. In "For Whom Things Did Not Change," Setu expresses her outrage: "It is good I never had a daughter. Because if I had had a daughter, and I knew a big man was doing unholy things with her, then with a matchet in my own hand, I would have cut that big man to pieces myself!"(11) And, given Aidoo's typically complex perspective, she has Setu identify other participants who are accountable for this moral disease corroding the social fabric—avaricious families who "try to profit by their daughters." Setu's strong condemnation is resounding: "I spit upon such big men! I spit upon such mothers! I spit upon such daughters!"(13)

In "Something to Talk About on the Way to the Funeral," two friends think back fondly of Auntie Araba's life, and are critical of the "educated big men" in their society who "have never been up to much good" (115). Education, rather than challenging patriarchal privilege, ironically reinforces it, for "was it not a lawyer-or-a-doctor-or something-like-that who was at the bottom of all Auntie Araba's troubles?" (119) This new educated class acquires a little learning and much more arrogance. When Ato, "this big scholar," gets Mansa pregnant, her "father nearly killed her" (120). Unfortunately, Mansa loses the opportunity to finish her schooling after the child is born, and as the storyteller remarks, "Mansa was a good girl. Not like one of these yetse-yetse things who think putting a toe in a classroom turns them into goddesses" (121).

Aidoo does not romanticize sexually objectified "girl-friends," nor does she regard them as victims. Rather, Aidoo recognizes the dilemma of being a woman in a changing patriarchal society. Mansa in "In the Cutting of a Drink" embraces prostitution amoralistically: "Any kind of work is work," she remarks to the narrator, who also learns that he must accept his sister's choice (37).

In urban areas, "big men" who have "girl-friends" indulge in visiting relationships that are very different from traditional polygamy that, with all its problems, requires male responsibility. There is no accountability for precarious sexual contacts; they are as unstable as the new fragile nation-states and their governments. Mercy's lover in "Two Sisters" is a powerful and rich politician when she takes up with him. When he is deposed in a coup, he becomes a nobody and Mercy changes allegiances to the newly powerful Captain Ashey. Even as she is complicitous in being sexually used by these "big men," she also relishes their power. Although Aidoo's representation makes such exploitative men accountable for their acts, she does not solely blame these men. She portrays women like Mercy, who use their bodies as weapons to acquire material wealth and to climb the social ladder.

In the same story, Connie, a respectable wife, also faces dilemmas of changing sexual mores in urban areas. She tolerates her husband's infidelities when she is pregnant with their second child. His reaction during her first pregnancy, even though he regrets it later, is strikingly abusive: "During her first pregnancy, he kept saying after the third month or so that the sight of her tummy the last thing before he slept always gave him nightmares" (97).

The particular dilemmas of mothers figure into a remarkable cluster of stories: a traditional child-custody dispute in "No Sweetness Here," the repeated burden of childbearing in "A Gift from Somewhere," and the comfort of children when men leave wives to a life of loneliness in "Certain Winds from the South." The narrator of "No Sweetness Here" is a respected local teacher, and as an outsider, she can look into village disputes objectively. She can also break certain communal codes such as the "indecent" act of dwelling upon "a boy's beauty." But, "Kwesi's beauty was indecent," she adds logically (57).

This title story is placed carefully in the middle of the collection as though Aidoo is making certain that her reader-listener has already been sensitized through the preceding stories. Kwesi's mother, Maami Ama, decides to face a formal divorce despite the risk of losing custody of her only son. She gets no support against her husband's abuse. Though her own mother tells her that "in marriage, a woman must sometimes be a fool," Maami Ama decides to fight back: "I have been a fool for far too long a time" (61).

"A Gift from Somewhere" draws a circle in the opposite direction from "No Sweetness Here," beginning with potential death and ending with life and hope. And in "Certain Winds from the South," Aidoo uses a striking narrative technique to convey women's loneliness when abandoned by their husbands, who are lured away from their villages to the south to earn a living. As M'ma Asana talks aloud, or contemplates in silence, other characters are given life through her words and thoughts. Aidoo uses this dramatic device where one actor takes on various roles, where one body embodies other voices and gestures. This is a strategy different from the one used in "No Sweetness Here." There, many characters speak in their own voices to express their views about who should get custody of Kwesi—his mother, his father's family, the teacher, and the general community. It is especially important for all to speak in their own voices because the teacher-narrator is an outsider, and perhaps she might misunderstand their customs. Also, as an educated woman she is set apart from the village folk.

But in "Certain Winds from the South," M'ma Asana tells the story and speaks the responses of other characters. For instance, when her husband leaves Hawa and her newborn son, Fuseni, M'ma has to convey the news:

> `Hawa, ah-ah, are you crying? Why are you crying? That your husband has left you to go and work . . . I do not understand, you say? Maybe I do not . . . See, now you have woken up Fuseni. Sit down and feed him and listen to me . . .
>
> Listen to me and I will tell you of another man who left his newborn child and went away.
>
> Did he come back? No, he did not come back. But do not ask me any more questions for I will tell you all' (52).

M'ma's story is meant to infuse new strength into Hawa so that she can care for her child and not grieve about losing her husband. Like mother, like daughter, their difficult destiny repeats itself, and the women manage to live with dignity, to overcome loneliness, and to rear strong children.

Aidoo ends her collection in the United States, where Kofi in "Other Versions," far away from home, gains an understanding of his mother's generosity. After a dinner party during which he feels that he is the main meal being consumed, he meets an African-American woman, Mrs. Hye, the hired kitchen help. Something triggers empathetic feelings in Kofi that he cannot articulate or verbalize until a few days later, in a subway, when he sees another "old or middle-aged" black woman (133). Kofi's heart goes out to her, as, initially, without words, some connection to a common ancestry leaps out at him. And for Kofi, more personally, these black women connect him with his Ghanaian mother: "I don't know what made me. But I drew out my wallet. I had received money from my scholarship. So I took some dollar bills, crumpled them in my hand and jumped like one goaded with a firebrand." He tells her, "'I come from Africa and you remind me of my mother. Please would you take this from me?'" (134)

When Kofi tells her that he is a student, she remarks, "'Son, keep them dollars. I sure know you need them more than I do.'" Kofi thinks, "Of course, she was Mother," a caring, nurturing spirit that had guided Kofi throughout his life (134).

The key in dilemma tales is discussion, almost a democratic process of listening to different points of view on a single subject, turning it around as as if viewing the shifting colored pieces of glass in a revolving kaleidoscope. Characteristically, the endings are often open-ended, as in "Everything Counts." The point of open-ended resolutions is that Aidoo makes the reader-listener an active participant in resolving the dilemma presented by that tale. Her technique is reminiscent of the Brechtian impulse to make the audience think as well as be entertained.

Other endings come to rest in death, as Kwesi's by snakebite, and despite the mother's heartbreaking sorrow at this irredeemable loss, the ending indicates that she will find the strength to go on. Mami Fanti endures three infant deaths and then savors the miraculous survival of her son Nyamekye in "A Gift from Somewhere." A different kind of death is depicted in that of Auntie Araba, a respected elder whose funeral is attended by the community and whose legacy of baking is carried on somewhat differently by her daughter-in-law, Mansa, who can now "bake hundreds of loaves of bread an hour with machines" (125).

Birth and death, youth and old age, wives, mothers, husbands, black masters and black servants, the exploitive new class of government ministers, the arrogant educated class versus wise elders who cannot read or write, storytellers and community listeners and participants—all find a place in Aidoo's universe, and all are portrayed with a loving though searing honesty. Aidoo represents her people with grave sympathy. They are not victims; they resist oppression where they can, and they discuss their deeply personal dilemmas, which have national import. Even as her vision encompasses political scenarios of corruption and "big men" exploiting unnamed mistresses, she never loses sight of the individuals inhabiting her narrative world. The relentless contempt and disgust that Ayi Kwei Armah portrays in his novel about contemporary Ghana, *The Beautyful Ones Are Not Yet Born,* do not figure into Aidoo's world. She can be as tough a critic of corruption as Armah, but she cares for her community and does not view its problems as beyond redemption. There is hope and struggle even when the sweetness vanishes.

The (In)Visibility of African Women Writers

Ever since I discovered Aidoo's stories in 1982 when I was preparing a lecture called "African Women Writers and Their Invisibility" for a women's studies brown-bag lunch at Yale University, I have loved these tales that resonate deeply with my own years of growing up in postcolonial India in the 1950s. For over ten years now, I have included Aidoo's stories in my undergraduate and graduate courses in African literature, postcolonial women writers, and contemporary fiction; they are as fresh now as when I first read them. And my students' readings are filled with discovery. Often, an Aidoo story with its depth, complexity, yet remarkably unponderous qualities has served to set up the ground for discussions of colonial history and gender roles amid changing neocolonial realities. Often, I have taught "Everything Counts" and "For Whom Things Did Not Change" along with sections of Fanon's *The Wretched of the Earth.*

Within the African literary tradition, male writers like

151

Afterword

Chinua Achebe and Wole Soyinka in Nigeria came to prominence first in the 1960s, even though women writers like Flora Nwapa in Nigeria and Aidoo in Ghana, whose careers span over three decades, were also writing at the time. One key manifestation of rendering women writers insignificant is to render them out of print, as in Aidoo's case. All of her work of the 1970s has been unavailable in the United States until the recent reissuing of her two dramas by Longman, the 1993 publication of *Changes* by The Feminist Press, and this very welcome republication of her short stories. Since *No Sweetness Here* has not been in print in the United States since the Anchor Doubleday edition of 1972,[5] it was not possible to teach the text in its entirety (as I often do with Bessie Head's rich volume of stories, *The Collector of Treasures*) as it well deserves to be taught, in order to demonstrate the range of Aidoo's themes and narrative techniques, and the structure and arrangement of the tales. Now, these stories can be included for serious study in school and college curricula. Readers can enjoy Aidoo's artistry, her subtle ironies, her evocations of Akan storytelling forms, her complex vision, and her refusal to provide simple answers to complex problems facing Ghanaian postcolonial society.

Another way to neglect women writers is to give them no serious critical attention. As Lloyd Brown remarks, "Western male Africanists have contributed heavily to an old boy network of African studies in which the African woman simply does not exist as a serious or significant writer" (5). Aidoo's literary productions since 1964 had not been studied in book form until Vincent O. Odamtten's recent, very worthwhile critical study entitled *The Art of Ama Ata Aidoo: Polylectics and Reading Against Neocolonialism*. In *Ngambika: Studies of Women in African Literature*, Carole Boyce Davies asserts the need for serious reevaluations of women writers who have often been dismissed casually by a male literary establishment. Constructive criticism is crucial in the development of any literary tradition. In a 1986 interview with Adeola James, Aidoo comments on the African woman writer's neglect and why there are no "female Achebes":

> The question of the woman writer's voice being muted
> has to do with the position of women in society generally.
> Women writers are just receiving the writer's version of
> the general neglect and disregard that woman in the larg-
> er society receives. I want to make that very clear. It is not
> unique. Now, as to the issue of where the female Achebes
> and so on are, you know that the assessment of a writer's
> work is in the hands of critics and it is the critics who put
> people on pedestals or sweep them under the carpet, or
> put them in a cupboard, lock the door and throw the key
> away. I feel that, wittingly or unwittingly, people may be
> doing this to African women writers; literally locking us
> out, because either they don't care or they actively hate us.
> Bessie Head died of neglect. So how is she going to be an
> Achebe? When nobody gives recognition to her as Bessie
> Head, as a woman in her own right trying to write—heh!
> *writing*—something relevant and meaningful?
> (Original emphasis, James 1990, 11–12)

In her autobiographical piece, "To Be a Woman,"
described by Allan as "a manifesto of African feminism" (171),
Aidoo comments on the pain she felt when *Our Sister Killjoy* was
ignored by Ghanaian critics:

> If *Killjoy* has received recognition elsewhere, it is gratify-
> ing. . . . But that is no salve for the hurt received because
> my own house has put a freeze on it. For surely my broth-
> ers know that the only important question is the critical
> recognition of a book's existence—not necessarily appro-
> bation. Writers, artists, and all who create, thrive on con-
> troversy. When a critic refuses to talk about your work,
> that is violence; he is willing you to die as a creative per-
> son" ("To Be a Woman," 262).

Afterword

Killjoy was not appreciated locally, since in it Aidoo exposes several discomforting truths about contemporary African society. She boldly satirizes the "black skin, white mask" bourgeois class of African leaders:

> Excellent idea . . .
> How can a
> Nigger rule well
> Unless his
> Balls and purse are
> Clutched in
> Expert White Hands? . . .
> Champagne sipping
> Ministers and commissioners
> Sign away
> Mineral and timber
> Concessions, in exchange for
> Yellow wheat which
> The people can't eat . . .
> While on the market place,
> The good yams rot for
> Lack of transportation . . .
> Our representatives and interpreters . . .
> maintain themselves on our backs (*Killjoy,* 56–58).

Aidoo's creative work and her statements in essays and interviews contribute significantly to the parameters of African feminism. Aidoo remarks that

> When people ask me rather bluntly every now and then whether I am a feminist, I not only answer yes, but I go on to insist that every woman and every man should be a feminist—especially if they believe that Africans should take charge of our land, its wealth, our lives, and the bur-

154

den of our own development. Because it is not possible to advocate independence for our continent without also believing that African women must have the best that the environment can offer. For some of us, this is the crucial element of our feminism ("The African Woman Today," 323).

Aidoo is an astute critic of the many cultural and economic issues facing her society. Moreover, her historical vision enables her to situate such creative representations within Africa's long, often bitter encounter with European colonizers and with continuing imperialist controls. Even as she honestly faces the many sociocultural situations where "sweetness" has vanished, Aidoo finds a way to retain a sympathetic and loving concern for the people who inhabit her world. The image of "sweetness" rolls on one's tongue as, along with Sissie on her returning flight to Africa, we also land on African soil guided so ably, even wittily, by Aidoo. Sissie's words towards the end of *Killjoy* embody a warmth and realism towards home: "She was back in Africa. And that felt like fresh honey on the tongue: a mixture of complete sweetness and smoky roughage. Below was home with its unavoidable warmth and even after these thousands of years, its uncertainties. 'Oh, Africa. Crazy old continent. . . .' Sissie wondered whether she had spoken aloud to herself" (133). When Aidoo speaks to us, her readers and listeners, her insights bring new illuminations and discoveries about the people who inhabit her stories and about their struggles and triumphs.

NOTES

1. For more detailed discussion of the economic and political impacts of colonization on African societies, see Basil Davidson, *Which Way Africa? The Search for a New Society* (Harmondsworth, U.K.: Penguin, 1973); Walter Rodney, *How Europe Underdeveloped Africa* (Washington D.C.: Howard University Press, 1974, reprint 1982).

Afterword

More specifically, for the impacts of colonization on African women, see Maria Cutrufelli, *Women of Africa: Roots of Oppression* (London: Zed Press, 1983), especially chapter 1, "Colonization and Social Change"; Edna Bay and Nancy Hafkin, eds., *Women in Africa: Studies in Social and Economic Change* (Stanford: Stanford University Press, 1976); Christine Obbo, *African Women: Their Struggle for Economic Independence* (London: Zed Press,1980); Ifi Amadiume, *Male Daughters, Female Husbands: Gender and Sex in an African Society* (London: Zed Press, 1987); Claire Robertson and Iris Berger, eds., *Women and Class in Africa* (New York and London: Africana Publishing Company,1986).

2. Frantz Fanon, *The Wretched of the Earth*, trans. Constance Farrington (New York: Grove Press, 1963; reprint 1991). See especially chapter 1, "Concerning Violence."

3. This is also reminiscent of the problematic word "postcolonial," which carries the baggage of colonialism. As Nayantara Sahgal, a writer from India, asked at a recent Commonwealth Literature Conference, "When will we be post-postcolonial?"

4. Aidoo records with biting humor how her expertise at using the English language was described by a student as "absolutely masculine." In a "Dialogue, May 1980," Aidoo reflects on this sexist remark which also evokes the colonial past and the neocolonial present: "I fold back into myself. I who am yet to find me on the graph of 'speakers of English as a second language,' or where I stand as a 'nonnative' user of the English language. At least once in the lifetime of a [post]colonial, there is a confrontation with the remark: `But you speak English . . . like an Englishman' . . . One's feelings at such times are ambivalent enough. Now I speak English like a man?" ("To Be A Woman," 261).

5. This 1972 edition was reviewed with a brief comment by Jan Carew in the *New York Times Book Review: "No Sweetness Here . . .* give[s] the reader gentle, polished but profound and ironic insights into the manner, morals, and esthetic sensibilities of contemporary West African society." Carew notes the "muted irony" of the stories and how they "nudge [the reader] quietly toward a more profound understanding of modern Africa" (14).

The first edition (1970) was reviewed by K.W. in *West Africa* (30 January 1971): "[These] short stories, like the play *[Anowa]*, are simple and direct, being concerned with the real problems of ordinary people. . . . Ama Ata writes with transparent honesty" (133).

SELECTED BIBLIOGRAPHY

Primary Works by Aidoo and Selected African Women Writers

Aidoo, Ama Ata. *Anowa*. London: Longman, 1970.

———. *Changes: A Love Story*. London: The Women's Press, 1991; New York: The Feminist Press, 1993, with an afterword by Tuzyline Jita Allan. Translated as *Forandringer en kjærlighetshistorie* by Toril Hanssen. Oslo: Tiden Norsk Forlag, 1993.

———. *The Dilemma of a Ghost*. London: Longman, 1965.

———. "No Saviours." *African Writers on African Writing*. Ed. G. D. Killam. Evanston, Ill.: Northwestern University Press, 1973.

———. *Our Sister Killjoy or Reflections from a Black-Eyed Squint*. London: NOK Publishers, 1979.

———. *Someone Talking to Sometime*. Harare, Zimbabwe: The College Press, 1985.

———. "To Be a Woman." *Sisterhood Is Global*. Ed. Robin Morgan. New York: Anchor Press, 1985.

———. "To Be an African Woman—An Overview and a Detail." *Criticism and Ideology: Second African Writers' Conference, Stockholm, 1986*. Ed. Kirsten Holst Petersen. Uppsala, Sweden: Scandinavian Institute of African Studies, 1988.

———. "The African Woman Today." *Dissent* 39 (1992): 319–25.

Bruner, Charlotte, ed. *Unwinding Threads: Writing by Women in Africa*. London: Heinemann, 1983.

Dangarembga, Tsitsi. *Nervous Conditions*. London: The Women's Press, 1988; Seattle: Seal Press, 1989.

Emecheta, Buchi. *The Joys of Motherhood*. New York: Braziller, 1979.

———. *The Slave Girl*. London: Allison & Busby, 1977.

Afterword

Gordimer, Nadine. *July's People*. London: Penguin, 1981; reprint 1986.

Head, Bessie. *A Question of Power*. London: Heinemann, 1974.

———. *The Collector of Treasures*. London: Heinemann, 1977.

———. *Tales of Tenderness and Power*. London: Heinemann, 1989.

———. *When Rain Clouds Gather*. London: Heinemann, 1968.

Nwapa, Flora. *Efuru*. London: Heinemann, 1966; reprint 1979.

Tlali, Miriam. *Soweto Stories*. London: Pandora Press, 1989.

Secondary Sources

Achebe, Chinua. "Impediments to Dialogue Between North and South." *Hopes and Impediments: Selected Essays*. New York: Anchor Press, 1988.

———. *Morning Yet on Creation Day*. New York: Anchor Press, 1976.

Amadiume, Ifi. *Male Daughters and Female Husbands: Gender and Sex in African Society*. London and New Jersey: Zed Press, 1987.

African Literature Today 15. Special Issue on African Women Writers. London: Heinemann, 1985.

Amos, Valerie, and Pratibha Parmer. "Challenging Imperial Feminism." *Feminist Review* 17 (Autumn 1984): 3-20.

Ashcroft, Bill, Gareth Griffiths, and Helen Tiffin, eds. *The Empire Writes Back: Theory and Practice in Post-Colonial Literatures*. London and New York: Routledge, 1989.

Barrett, Michelle. *Women's Oppression Today: Problems in Marxist Feminist Analysis*. London: Verso, 1980.

Brown, Lloyd W. *Women Writers in Black Africa*. Westport, CT: Greenwood Press, 1981.

Carew, Jan. "African Literature—From the Breath of Gods." *The New York Times Book Review*. 2 April 1972, pp. 7,14.

Davies, Carole Boyce, and Anne Adams Graves, eds. *Ngambika: Studies of Women in African Literature*. Trenton, NJ: Africa World Press, 1986.

Fanon, Frantz. *The Wretched of the Earth*. Trans. Constance Farrington.

New York: Grove Press,1961; reprint 1977.

Hafkin, Nancy and Edna Bay, eds. *Women in Africa: Studies in Social and Economic Change.* Stanford: Stanford University Press, 1976.

Hill-Lubin, Mildred. "The Storyteller and the Audience in the Works of Ama Ata Aidoo." *Neohelicon* 26, no. 2 (1989): 221–45.

James, Adeola, ed. *In Their Own Voices: African Women Writers Talk.* London: Heinemann, 1990.

Jayawardena, Kumari. *Feminism and Nationalism in the Third World.* London: Zed Press, 1986.

Katrak, Ketu H. "Decolonizing Culture: Towards a Theory for Postcolonial Women Writers." *Modern Fiction Studies* 35, no. 1 (Spring 1989): 157–79.

———. "From Paulina to Dikeledi: "The Philosophical and Political Vision of Bessie Head's Protagonists." *Ba Shiru* 12, no. 2 (1987): 26–35.

Lazarus, Neil. *Resistance in Postcolonial African Fiction.* New Haven, CT: Yale University Press, 1990.

Little, Kenneth. *The Sociology of Urban Women's Image in African Literature.* Totowa, NJ: Rowman and Littlefield, 1980.

McCaffrey, Kathleen. "Images of the Mother in the Stories of Ama Ata Aidoo." *Africa Woman* 23 (Sept./Oct. 1979): 40–41.

Modebe, Sarah. "Ama Ata Aidoo—In Conversation." *New African* 288 (Sept. 1991): 40.

Mohanty, Chandra et al, eds. *Third World Women and the Politics of Feminism.* Bloomington, IN: Indiana University Press, 1990.

Ngugi wa Thiong'o. *Decolonizing the Mind: The Politics of Language in African Literature.* London: Heinemann, 1986.

Nasta, Susheila, ed. *Motherlands: Black Women's Writing from Africa, the Caribbean and South Asia.* London: The Women's Press, 1991.

Obbo, Christine. *African Women: Their Struggle for Economic Independence.* London: Zed Press, 1980.

Odamtten, Vincent O. *The Art of Ama Ata Aidoo: Polylectics and Reading Against Neocolonialism.* Gainesville, FL: University Press of Florida, 1994.

Afterword

Pala, Achola. "Women and Development." *The Black Woman Cross-Culturally*. Ed. Filomena Steady. Cambridge, MA: Schenkman, 1981.

Pieterse, Cosmo and Dennis Duerden. *African Writers Talking*. New York: Africana Publishing, 1972.

Priebe, Richard K., ed. *Ghanaian Literatures*. Westport, CT: Greenwood Press, 1988.

Soyinka, Wole. *Art, Dialogue and Outrage: Essays on Literature and Culture*. Ibadan, Nigeria: New Horn Press, 1988.

Terborg-Penn, Rosalyn et al, eds. *Women in Africa and the African Diaspora*. Washington D.C.: Howard University Press, 1989.